MW00795757

DECEPTION BAY

CHRIS PATCHELL

PRAISE FOR CHRIS PATCHELL

"A fun, crisply written page turner that had me guessing until the end!"

"All in all, another wonderfully entertaining story from this author..."

"Deception Bay, by Chris Patchell is fabulous. I immediately fell in love with the main character, Austin Martell."

"Seriously, creative and engaging, indeed."

"This is a fast, short, easy read full of twists and turns."

"Interesting and involving story of discovery and self-improvement."

Copyright © 2018 by Chris Patchell
All rights reserved.

No part of this book may be reproduced in any form or by any electronic or
mechanical means, including information storage and retrieval systems, without
written permission from the author, except for the use of brief quotations in a book
review.

This book is a work of fiction. Characters, incidents, places and dialogue are drawn
from the author's imagination or are used fictitiously and are not to be construed as
real. Any resemblance to actual events, locales, or persons, living or dead, is entirely
coincidental.

❀ Created with Vellum

This book is for my good friend Don, who introduced me to the magic of Whidbey Island and with whom I've shared so many adventures... and martinis.

PROLOGUE

The howling wind drives the steep waves toward the boat. A huge swell hits. White spray cannons over the bow. The hull shudders from the impact. Ice cold water sluices across the deck. Panic writhes like a live current inside him. He's sailed through summer storms before, though none as fierce as this. *Think. Think*, he commands himself, marshalling his fear.

Reduce the sail.

He pulls a jack knife from his pocket and saws through the rope securing the jib. The sail lets go. It flutters and snaps like a wild thing in the blustering storm. Another wave crests over the bow, washing away the lingering traces of blood.

The boat shudders. Chest heaving, he sheathes the knife and drops to his hands and knees while all around him the wind howls, the relentless waves roar.

Lower the mainsail.

He inches along the deck until he reaches the base of the mast and arches up to lower the sail.

The wind snakes across the waves and catches hold of the boom. It jibes with brutal force and slams into his shoulder in a blinding flash of pain. He sprawls to the deck. The scream of the splitting metal hinge sounds as the gooseneck rips free. The boom flails above.

He's lost control.

The deck tilts and he's sliding—careening toward the edge. He screams. His hands scrabble desperately, searching for something to grab onto, to stop himself from plunging over the side into the churning black sea.

His fingers graze a rope and he grabs hold. Hand over hand, he hauls himself up the deck, muscles straining as the next wave hits. The storm is intensifying.

He needs to get below deck.

The boat pitches and he loses his footing as he scrambles toward the cabin's opening. He grabs hold of the ladder and climbs down into the darkness below. The water is already thigh-deep—as heavy as wet cement as he struggles toward the red light.

The radio.

Teeth chattering, he drives his legs forward. Stumbling. Reaching. Gasping until he makes it. He tears the microphone from its perch. Thumbs the button. He screams out the words in a torrent of panic, hoping somebody will hear.

"Mayday! Mayday! Mayday! This is the *Dreamcatcher*. We're three miles east of Deception Bay. We are sinking. Repeat. We are sinking. One on board, one overboard. Over."

One overboard... Scott. He can't think about that now.

Dropping the radio, he lunges forward and falls to his knees. Hands scrabbling across the floor, he searches for the seacock located on the hull. His shaking fingers clutch the lever. It's stuck. He clenches his teeth and tries twisting it again. Harder. Heart booming.

The boat must sink. It's his only hope.

The valve gives way and opens, filling the ship like a well. A flash of lightning illuminates the cabin. The water is hip-deep now. He bats away the floating seat cushions on his way toward the ladder.

A wave smashes into the side of the hull. The boat heaves. It rises on the swell, yawing sideways, exposing it to the steep wave. Then it rolls.

Cast violently onto his side, he struggles to get his bearings as seawater surges into the small cabin. It happens fast. The hull fills until he is completely submerged. He pumps his arms and legs, aiming for the opening, desperate to swim out. But the life vest strapped around his chest keeps pulling him up, pinning him, trapping him inside the dying boat.

His lungs burn—screaming for air.

He needs out.

Numb fingers fumble with the straps securing the vest. They are sticky. Stubborn. He grabs for the jack knife. Cuts it free.

Desperate—terrified, he swims toward the opening until he is out. Breaking the surface, he comes up beside the boat and gasps in the salty air. He spies a life ring floating a few feet away and surges toward it.

He grabs hold of the orange ring as the black water crashes overhead in a bone-chilling embrace, forcing him down. He kicks his feet, driving upward, clinging to the life ring with all he's got. Waves pummel him from all sides. For the first time since he was an altar boy at his grandmother's church, he prays.

Please God. Please God. Please God.

God never answered his prayers back then. Why should he now? After what he's done...

He mouths the words of the rosary prayer as the minutes drag past. Pummeled by the frigid waves, each second is excruciating. A clock ticks down in his mind. Ten minutes. Maybe less before hypothermia sets in.

The boat is gone. He's going to die. He clings stubbornly to the life ring, unwilling to give up.

Suddenly, a noise breaks overhead. Deep. Deafening. The *thud, thud* of helicopter blades. Casting a desperate gaze skyward, he is trapped in a blinding circle of light. He squints. Freeing one arm from the life ring, he waves it frantically overhead at the Coast Guard chopper hovering above.

1

My head pounds from the river of martinis I consumed just a few short hours ago. I peek through the window of the 747 and wince as the golden orange glow of the rising sun hits me square in the eyes with all the force of a seagull sucked into a turbine. I close my eyes, and like Neo, from *The Matrix*, I find myself wishing I'd taken the blue pill instead of the red one.

Why, oh why, oh why, did I take the call?

Just as plain as the spots on the inside of my eyelids, I can see Diana's sober expression as she thrust the phone in my face.

"Austin, you need to take this," she said.

I pulled the phone from her bony, talon-like grip, because in the five years I've been with the Writer's Place Literary Agency, I *always* do what Diana tells me. Well, okay. That's not universally true. It's more accurate to say I *should always* do everything Diana tells me. I've lived to regret the few times I chose not to heed her advice.

And just like that, the fleeting high from standing center stage at my own book launch party fizzled like bubbles in flat champagne. Now, here I sit, strapped into a seat so uncomfortably narrow that even a Russian gymnast would complain, chasing the light of dawn across the continent to the last place in the world I'd ever want to go.

Home.

I can think of a dozen gooey, heartwarming quotes about homecomings and wallowing in the heart of familial bliss. None of them speak to me. I think Thomas Wolfe had it right when he said, "You can never go home again."

I've had twenty-eight hundred miles and six hours to mull over how *can* and *should* are two very different things.

EVEN AT THIS ungodly time of day, SeaTac Airport swarms with life. Natural light floods through the massive windows and nearly blinds me. I don my sunglasses and follow the throng of fellow travelers toward baggage claim.

I catch sight of my reflection in the glass window of a storefront as I pass by and slow down for a better look. I stroke the short beard covering my jaw and grin. Considering I spent the night on a plane, I look damned good.

The window ends, and I scan the racks of books at Hudson's News. And there it is, big as life. I stop dead in my tracks. Displayed right out in front is my new novel, *Murder at Echo Lake*. You know, I never get tired of seeing my name in print. There it is in 120-point gold type.

Apparently, you need to signal when you stop, because just then, someone slams into me and I stagger a step to regain my balance. The man turns, his red face apologetic.

"Sorry. Are you okay?"

I nod and keep walking.

People on the West Coast are way nicer than they are back east. In New York I'd be yelled at, and flipped off, probably with some nasty slur about my mother. But here, they apologize. Weird.

Halfway down the terminal, I see a happy sight. The green goddess on the Starbucks sign beckons me, and my feet, as if on autopilot, steer me to her.

The aroma of roasting coffee beans smells deep and earthy, like salvation, and I'm standing in line when my cell phone rings. I dig in my pockets until I find it. Heads swivel in my direction as the theme song to the movie *Jaws* plays. With a grin, I pick up the call.

"Where did you disappear to last night?"

My agent, Diana Black, sounds as irritated as a cranky toddler.

"Good morning to you too, sunshine."

"Did you leave with the blonde or the brunette?"

I smile as I contemplate the question. Most of my loyal readers fit a certain demographic. Many came of age in the days of JFK and Martin Luther King. Occasionally, though, I meet fans who are more, shall we say, in keeping with my particular tastes.

Anyway, the fact that Diana is asking about my love life has me intrigued. She hasn't shown the slightest romantic interest in me since Chicago, five years ago. And to be perfectly honest, there wasn't much romance that night.

"Austin," she prompts me.

Did I mention Diana's pathological hatred for pauses? Life moves at warp speed for her. I suppose that's probably true of most successful literary agents. I drag the pause out for a second or two longer before I answer.

"Both."

"Both. Really?"

She sounds surprised, and maybe a little disconcerted. I find myself wishing I could see her expression. By the sound of her voice, I think she's frowning, but I can't tell for sure.

"No," I say vaguely, enjoying her stunned silence a little too much. Finally, I relent and tell her the truth. "I'm in Seattle."

"Seattle?" she barks into the phone. I wince as the sound pierces my eardrum like an ice pick. "What the hell are you doing in Seattle?"

The coffee line shifts and I'm next up for that magic, caffeinated elixir I need to fuel me. A few fitful hours of sleep on a plane won't be enough to steel me for a fiery reentry into my past.

"My mother was hurt in an accident."

I count to three as I wait for Diana to respond. Three seconds is a lifetime for her. Finally, she speaks.

"I'm sorry to hear that."

"Not half as sorry as I am."

"How bad is it?"

"Well, she's not going to play the violin again," I say, but Diana doesn't laugh. "I don't know yet."

"Couldn't you hire a nurse?"

I snort. Family obligations don't rate high on Diana's priority list. This is one of the many ways in which she and I are alike.

"Believe me, the thought crossed my mind."

"And?"

"And honestly, my mother is..." I lift my hand in a palms-up gesture and grasp for the right word. I write for a living, for God's sake; describing my own mother's personality quirks shouldn't be that hard. Unfortunately, I've been raised well enough to realize that it's impolite to call your own mother a sociopath, to anyone other than a therapist, that is. "She's difficult."

I can almost hear Diana rolling her eyes.

"I hate to break it to you, Austin, but all mothers are difficult."

"Yeah, well, mine's something special."

I trail off when I hear Diana sigh. I can picture her shaking her head, her dark eyebrows pinched so tightly together they almost touch.

"Okay. How long will you be in Seattle?"

"About an hour. I'm actually heading to Whidbey Island."

"Where?" she groans. "Whatever. When will you be back in New York?"

"A week. Maybe two."

She sucks in a breath of air like she's been sucker-punched, and I know she's trying not to lose her shit. And I know why.

"Two weeks? You're scheduled to go on book tour in ten days."

"I know."

The Starbucks line shifts again, and suddenly it's my turn. Talking on a cell phone and holding up a line is considered a cardinal sin back in New York. Seriously, it's grounds for murder in my neigh-borhood. The barista, a doe-eyed, teenage girl, smiles wider than a

Miss Teen USA contestant, and I'm momentarily blinded by the glare from her unnaturally white teeth.

"Welcome to Starbucks," she says. "What can I get for you?"

I blink. She might be the sweetest Starbucks barista I've ever met.

"Austin," Diana barks.

"Just a second."

I scan the menu for the strongest drink they have. Strong coffee with a shot of espresso. That has to be a winner, right?

"I'll have a red eye."

Okay, it's a little cliché, and behind me, I hear a cacophony of groans, but the barista giggles like it's the funniest thing she'd heard all day. Her hazel eyes dance with light. I might just love her.

"One shot or two?"

"Two. No, three."

I hold up three fingers and she nods like the good girl she is.

"Yes, sir."

Sir. She called me sir. Charmed, I hand over my debit card. I'm half-tempted to prolong the transaction, since this might be the last pleasant conversation I have for the next few weeks, or however long it's going to take me to sort my mother out. I feel a keen stab of disappointment when she hands back my card, and I shuffle to the end of the counter to wait.

"One week. Promise me you'll be back by then," Diana says.

"I pinkie promise."

Diana doesn't say goodbye. She hangs up with a grunt, and I stow my phone as the barista calls my drink.

"Red eye."

She sets the coffee cup down with a grin, and I snatch it off the countertop. Lava hot coffee sloshes over the side and I hiss, instinctively sticking my finger in my mouth and sucking on the burn. Moments later, I slide it into a sleeve before merging back into the human flow trudging toward baggage claim.

"One week," I mutter.

Ha! I'll kill myself if I stay a minute longer.

2

The growling engine emits a throaty purr as the ferry pushes away from the dock. A tremor shudders through the hull. I tense, buffeted by the waves of dread that wash over me.

Breathe, asshole.

For an islander, I have an unnatural fear of large bodies of water. Back in New York, I decline offers for dinner cruises. I avoid the Staten Island Ferry like the plague. Hell, I don't even like taking baths. My brother was the sailor in the family.

Scott.

A stab of pain at the unexpected thought of him pierces my heart. Fifteen years ago, I buried the horror of what happened as deep in my psyche as it would go. I will not let it consume me now.

I shift my focus away from my inner turmoil to the world outside. It's beautiful here—even a staunch New York vampire like me can see that. Beyond the window, Whidbey Island glimmers like an emerald set amid the deep blue of Puget Sound. With every thrust of the engine, the faint outline of the Seattle skyline shrinks in the distance.

I feel the last remnants of civilization slipping away and the insulated reality of my everyday life along with it. The ghosts on this island do not rest in peace, I fear. As the shoreline draws near, I feel them beginning to rise.

A bubble of panic expands inside my chest. Trapped in the confines of the ferry, it starts to grow. Sweat prickles along my hairline. I breathe deep, trying to dispel my burgeoning fear.

Washington State ferries are as safe as busses. More safe, as a matter of fact. Still, nightmare newsreel images of sinking ferries and drowning passengers soon fill the screaming vortex inside my mind.

Christ. Nothing bad is going to happen. It is a picture-perfect day.

It's true. I know it. But a sudden, fervent restlessness takes hold. I rise from my seat and stride toward the front of the ferry, driven by the faint hope that perhaps the fresh air blowing in my face might dispel the bout of nausea brewing at the pit of my gut. I push through the doors.

Golden sunlight bathes the deck. The breeze is cool, and I pull the salty air into my lungs. Leaning against the railing, I let it out. The sight of so much water fills me with dread, like at any moment an unseen hand might sweep me from the deck and drag me beneath the surface until my lungs fill and the world goes black. My gaze strays away from the stony island shore, to the murky blue of Puget Sound. Despite the late summer sun that beats down on my shoulders, I shiver.

The ocean isn't like the land. It is a living, breathing thing. It sighs, and heaves, surges, and writhes with life.

And death.

It was there, three miles east of Deception Bay, on a day much like this one, where my life was forever changed.

My heart beats faster, keeping time with my racing thoughts. My fingers curl around the iron railing in a death grip and I realize what a colossally stupid mistake I've made. I shouldn't have come out here. I should go back inside where it's warmer. Safer. But my feet refuse to budge.

The bubble of anxiety inside my chest bursts. I struggle to draw in a breath. It's no use. The darkness is closing in. I'm shaking. Sweating. My knees buckle, and I'm sinking to the deck.

I hear the distant, muted spike of alarm in the voices around me. The words are indistinct—the sound distorted, as if I've plunged beneath the frigid surface of Puget Sound.

"Hey."

I startle at the feel of warm fingers curling around my forearms. It's a woman. The faint floral scent of her perfume cuts through the briny breeze.

"It's okay," she says. "You're safe. Just focus on your breathing, slow and easy. Okay?"

I try to speak, but no sound emerges. I barely manage a nod.

"Maybe everyone can step back and give us some room."

Her voice is like a life ring amid the storm of panic. I cling to her soft, calming words. Little by little she draws me back into the sun. I open my eyes.

"Where are you from?" she asks.

"New York," I squeak, sounding like a middle-grader whose voice hasn't yet dropped.

"I love New York. It's been years since I've been there. Born and raised on the island, though. Whidbey will always be home. Is this your first time here?"

I draw in a shaky breath and focus on her. She's pretty. Oval face. Dark hair. Steady brown eyes.

"No...it's been...a long time."

"Well, it hasn't changed much. That's part of what I love about the place. Predictable. Definitely slower paced."

"Glacial," I add.

She laughs. It's a sweet, melodic sound that reminds me of wind chimes.

"Well, yeah. The slower pace of island life might be the kind of therapy a city boy like you needs."

I like her gently teasing tone and I flash a shaky grin. The engine drops in pitch. The wind dries the sweat on my brow, and my heart begins to slow.

"How are you feeling?"

"Better. Thank you."

"I'm Ellie."

"Austin," I say.

"Well, Austin, do you think you can stand?"

People are staring. A flush of shame rises up my neck as I avoid looking around. She pushes to her feet and offers her hands. And though I'm perfectly capable of standing on my own, I twine my fingers in hers. Her grip is strong. Shifting her weight back on her heels, she pulls, and I rise from the deck and start to feel like myself again.

"Was that the first panic attack you've had?"

"Not exactly. I once had an epic meltdown on the observation deck of the Empire State Building."

"Really?"

"I shrieked like a toddler. It took an entire precinct of NYPD officers to talk me down."

"You're joking."

"Would I lie to you?"

I smile directly into her lovely eyes. Suddenly aware that I'm still holding her hands, I release my grip. Not many people know that I suffered from horrible anxiety attacks the first year I lived in New York. Everything about the place induced another crushing wave of panic—the noise, the crowds, the pressure of exams, writing essays on dead poets, talking to a strange girl.

"Any idea what triggered this one?"

"The water."

"The water? And you're heading to an island?"

"I never said I was smart."

We both laugh at the irony of it. The wind blows her dark hair around her tanned cheeks, but Ellie doesn't seem to notice. She's so natural, so un-New York. I've never been attracted to the girl-next-door type, but I find myself mesmerized by her pretty smile.

The ferry horn blasts and I know we're close to our destination. A scratchy, near-unintelligible voice comes across the speakers. Riders scurry back down into the bowels of the vessel to their waiting cars.

Ellie glances over her shoulder, then back at me. She's going to leave me now. I shouldn't care, but for some odd reason I don't care to define, I do.

"So, Austin, you're going to be okay?"

"I don't know," I say, hitching my shoulder in a shrug. "As you pointed out, I'm on an island surrounded by water. It's not every day a guy gets rescued by a pretty woman. Maybe you should give me your number...you know...in case I have another emergency."

"Oh, don't worry. If you have another emergency, I'll find you."

I have no idea what that means, but before I can ask her to clarify, Ellie is gone.

3

I disembark the ferry along with all the other foot traffic. We pool into the pick-up area—a rag-tag group of hippie wannabes in their cargo shorts and Crocs, and me, the sophisticated urbanite wearing designer jeans and a Hugo Boss shirt.

Cars exit the ferry like bees emerging from a hive. I watch them stream up the hill, subtly hoping to catch a glimpse of Ellie, but no such luck. With the precision of a military parade, the next set of cars is loaded, and the ferry pulls away from the dock. I sit on the scarred wooden bench in the midday sun and wonder where the hell my ride is.

I booked a car from the plane, and though I got a confirmation, I'm still sitting here. I pull out my phone to check the time. Just my luck. It's totally fucking dead.

Exhausted from the nearly sleepless night I spent getting here, I slump down on the bench. With nothing to do but wait, I close my eyes and tilt my face up toward the sun. A fly buzzes around my head, and I shoo it away. God, it's so quiet out here, it's creepy. No horns blare, no sirens wail, the constant hum of traffic clogging the New York streets trickles down to a mere whisper on the island. It's like life after the zombie apocalypse—nothing but trees, and bugs.

My head tips back against the wall and I drift. I haven't thought about this place for years. Random memories of grassy fields, household chores, and long summer vacations drift through my mind.

I stay like this—inside my fuzzy Zen cocoon—until the ear-splitting blare of a car horn jars me awake.

The car. Finally.

With a silver hoop hanging from one ear and scruffy beard that has mostly run to gray, the driver looks like a modern-day pirate.

"Catching flies?" he calls through the open window.

"What?" I feign ignorance and straighten on the bench.

"At first I thought it was a cabezon sitting there."

A cabezon is a distant relative of a scorpion fish found in the Pacific Ocean. Only a local, or a marine biologist, would know that. This guy looks like he has more in common with Rob Zombie than Jacques Cousteau. I subtly swipe my hand across my mouth to brush away any lingering remnants of drool and rise from the bench. He exits the car.

"When I saw the name on the reservation, I almost didn't believe it. Austin Martell live and in the flesh. How the hell are ya?"

He sticks out his hand like we're old friends. And maybe we are. I've worked hard to forget this place. The puzzled look on my face gives me away, and he clasps my hand with a grin.

"Rob. Rob Fletcher, you big tool."

"Shit, Rob. I'm sorry. I didn't recognize you with the..."

I scratch the short beard covering my jaw.

"Yeah, everyone needs a hobby," he jokes as he strokes the unruly tangle of bristles on his chin.

Rob and I went to high school together and hung out in the same crowd. He thumps my shoulder, grabs my suitcase, and loads it into the trunk. Now that I realize I know him, it doesn't feel right to sit in the back. I pop open the passenger's door and climb inside.

"God, what's it been?" Rob asks as he slides the car into drive.

"Fifteen years."

"Christ on a cracker, Austin. What brings you back?"

"My mother had an accident."

"Aw, shit, I heard something about that. Is she going to be okay?"

"Not sure. I haven't made it to the hospital yet."

"Island Memorial?" he asks. I nod. "Okay, let's get you there."

He hammers on the gas and I'm pushed back into my seat as the car rockets up the hill. I glance in the side mirror and see the next group of cars queued up for boarding as the ferry dock disappears. The roads stretching out before us are as familiar as the lines in my hand, the map of my childhood indelibly burned into my memory.

Rob hits the brake suddenly to avoid a slower moving car, and my breath catches. He shakes his fist out the open window and curses at the driver as we scream past.

"Goddamned tourists. The island is full of them," Rob grumbles. "So, you're some kind of writer now, I hear."

"So they tell me."

"I still remember the story you wrote about the shark when we were in high school. Right then, I knew you would either become a writer or a florist. Even money on both sides," Rob jokes.

I chuckle. "So, what about you?"

"Two jobs. I work as a cook at the Willows. You remember the place. It's the resort outside of town. And this." He gestures to the car with a wry smile. "It's not much, but it's mine. I was never the type to work in an office."

I nod. "Wife? Kids?"

"Two of each. Of course, one of them is an ex. You remember her from high school. Tina Mason. Crazy girl. Great legs though."

I picture her—long blonde hair and freckled face. She spent her summer like half of the other island kids getting lit on the beach.

"Has it changed much? The island?"

"More Seattle assholes moving here every day."

I'm running out of small talk and we still have a ways to go before we reach the hospital in Coupeville.

"I don't suppose you have a cell phone charger?"

He fixes me with a shrewd grin and knocks his elbow on the armrest between us.

"Even savages like us have the internet and cell phone networks these days."

I open the compartment and sort through the cords to find one that fits. My phone beeps as I plug it in.

Acres of evergreen forests fly by in a blur, and I'm reminded again just how sparsely inhabited the island is. More people live in a Manhattan block than the towns of Freeland and Greenbank combined. As we pass the turn-off for Smuggler's Cove Road, my cell phone starts to ring. The theme song to *Jaws* plays.

"Aren't you going to answer it?"

"It's not safe to go in the water," I joke.

"Ah, your girlfriend."

"Worse." It's Diana. I pick up the call.

"Austin?"

"Live and in the flesh."

"I just got off the phone with the people at the Network."

"The Network?"

"You know, the Mystery Network, about the show."

I'm momentarily stunned into silence. Diana heaves a sigh.

"Seriously, Austin. We talked about it last night."

"Was that before or after I started drinking?" I can tell by the strained silence she's miffed. "Why don't you catch me up?"

"Their offer comes with a lot of zeros. Six in fact."

Suddenly, my mouth is too dry to whistle. I cluck my tongue in response.

"Damn."

"Is that a good damn or bad?"

"Good. How many seasons are we talking?"

"One for starters. After that, we'll see. But listen, Austin, there's a catch. They want another book. Fast. Get started right away on the outline and send me sample chapters. This week."

"You know I've got a lot going on here? With my mother dying and all?"

Okay, I'm being a tad melodramatic. I can picture Diana frowning on the other end of the call, and suddenly my head starts to pound. I need caffeine and sleep, not necessarily in that order. I need to get off the phone before she assigns me more work.

"I'll do my best, but I can't make any promises. It will depend on how things go."

"This is big money, Austin. Surely you can find some time to sit down with your laptop and crank out a few chapters."

Just like that, I think. Like it's easy. Like everyone can do it. Writing a story takes thousands of hours of writing and rewriting, and that's for professionals who have already honed their craft.

"Sure, Diana. Whatever."

"Whatever?"

Her voice rises in pitch and I can sense the escalating conflict. I'm in no shape to argue. And hey, if she's looking for me to rush some stuff to her, so be it. She'll get what she's asking for. Any hack can churn out shit.

"I said I'd do it."

"Call me tomorrow, Austin. I mean it."

"You always do."

I end the call and toss the phone into the cup holder and huff out an exasperated breath. Diana can really be a handful. Most of the time it works in my favor, but at times like this, her intensity is dialed up to eleven when I need her to be at a two.

"Dude, your wife is intense," Rob says.

"Not my wife. My agent."

I say it in a way that discourages further conversation on the topic. This chapter of my life includes seeing my mother, hiring a nurse, and getting the hell off the island before my book tour begins. Oh, and now to make matters worse, I need to pull a new book out of my ass.

Whatever. Tonight I'll crack open my laptop and get to work. Crank out some new pages. Send them to Diana. Problem is, I thought I was done with this series. I don't have another story idea lined up.

"Did I hear you say network?"

"It's preliminary stuff. These deals fall apart all the time."

Rob grunts and I can hear the wheels turning. Before nightfall, word of my new series will have spread across the island, and when it fails to materialize through no fault of my own, everyone will think it was bullshit.

We cross the town line into Coupeville. The place is even smaller than I remember it. Dollar store tourist shops and mangy pubs crowd the main drag. There are a few decent looking restaurants on the water front. Rolling down the window, I breathe in the salty air. Beyond the rooftops, I spy the bay.

Coupeville is located on the south end of Penn Cove, made famous for its mussels. I know restaurants in Manhattan that serve these things. We zip by the corner where Mark Hammer beat the hell out of me when I was eleven years old for doing something as stupid as accidentally tripping him in gym class. Okay, maybe it wasn't so accidental. It would have been worse if Scott hadn't come around the corner when he did. One look at my brother, the jock, sent Mark and his merry band of idiots on their way.

Nobody messed with Scott.

That last thought hits like a gut punch. I wish I was in my condo with a martini and my laptop, far away from this place and the memories it invokes.

The car grinds up the steep hill and I see Island Memorial dead ahead. I have a sudden, visceral reaction to the sight of it. Now that we're here, I realize that I am totally unprepared to face my mother.

4

"Dude, you look like you need a drink," Rob says, sliding the car into a parking spot and killing the engine.

"I wish."

"We could hit a pub at the bottom of the hill..."

"The Rabid Dog Saloon? No thanks. My shots aren't up to date."

Rob chuckles and shakes his head. "Gone all uppity on us?"

I don't answer. The tension in my shoulders ratchets another notch tighter.

The last time I spoke to my mother was Christmas Day. It was the kind of short, awkward, obligatory conversation you might have with a distant relative. I wasn't kidding when I said my mother was difficult. We haven't set eyes on each other since I left for college. But I hear her. She's the one inside the back of my mind telling me that I'm a loser, that no matter what I accomplish it will never be enough. Hell, even my shrink is afraid of her.

She always said that I was just like my father, but I don't remember him. He died on a fishing boat when I was a toddler. Now, I'm all she has left.

"You need a ride back to your mom's?" Rob asks.

"Yeah," I say, forcing myself to exit the car. "I'm not sure how long I'm going to be though."

"Text me when you're ready."

"You sure? Could be a while."

He shrugs. "What are friends for?"

Friends. I tuck his business card into my pocket and step outside.

My legs feel stiff from all the sitting as I walk through the sliding glass doors. And just like that, it's as if I've been transported back to my childhood. I spent more than my fair share of time getting patched up for whatever ill-fated adventure I'd embarked upon—a sprained ankle jumping hurdles in gym class, a broken arm falling out of a tree when I was spying on Scott, and the time I passed out while donating blood.

I stop by the information desk, where an older, white-haired woman sits.

"I'm looking for Linda Martell's room."

She looks up through the thick lenses of her glasses. A smile creases her face.

"Now, you must be Austin. I'm Mrs. Newman. I was your third-grade teacher."

"Oh, Mrs. Newman. Of course." I offer her my hand.

"I hear that you're a writer now. Imagine that."

"How is my mother?" I ask.

Her smile falters at the question. "I can't really say. Her room is down the hall. One-twenty. The doctor's doing rounds. If you hurry, you might catch him."

"Thank you."

I head down the hall, my mind spinning. The nurse on the phone told me that Mom fell and hit her head, that she was still unconscious, and that I needed to come. I was either too shocked or too drunk to ask questions, so now, I don't know what to expect. A swell of anxiety crests as I catch sight of a tall, thin man I assume to be the doctor.

A white lab coat billows around his button-down shirt and khaki pants. The harsh florescent lights shine off the bald spot peeking through the thinning hair at the crown of his freckled scalp.

"Doctor Alder," a nurse in blue scrubs calls out.

He looks up. A sudden jolt of recognition shoots through me. I didn't recognize Rob from my high school class, but this man I do know. He has a long face and a straight nose that has never once taken a hit. If it weren't for him, there is no way I would have passed high school science.

His exchange with the nurse is blessedly short. She peels off and I head straight for him.

"Doctor Alder? Who in their right mind would grant a medical license to a guy who blew up the chemistry lab?"

His look of surprise turns into a grin, and he tucks the file under his arm with a laugh.

"Don't let the stethoscope fool you, I got my medical certification through an online Guatemalan school. As for the ill-fated science experiment, I'm not the one who tossed potassium into the fish tanks."

We shake hands like grown-ups.

"I hear you're a *New York Times* bestselling author now."

"I don't know what you've heard, but if it's good, then I guarantee every word of it is true."

"You always could spin a tale," he says.

"What can I say? Some artists work in oils, I work in bullshit."

Stephen laughs again. He's got this deep, horsey laugh that turns heads. Even now, it's endearing.

"So, how's Mom?"

Stephen's smile fades and my heart drops.

"She took quite a blow to the head."

"Blow to the head? Her fall, you mean?"

Stephen shrugs. "The location and nature of her injuries aren't consistent with a fall."

I blink, trying to absorb the shock of what Stephen has just said. If not a fall, then what?

"You haven't spoken to the police?" he asks.

I shake my head. My cell phone was either off or dead for most of the trip.

"Chief Sharpe can fill you in on the investigation. We've done some tests, but we'll know more in the next day or two when she wakes up."

"She hasn't woken up?"

A sense of foreboding presses down on me. Sure, we weren't close, but she is my mother. My only family.

Stephen gives my shoulder a friendly squeeze. "Try not to worry, Austin. We're taking good care of her."

"Thank you."

We shake hands again and he walks away.

Apprehension slows my tread as I approach her door. This is not how I imagined things. I fully expected to find Mom awake and chomping at the bit to get out of here. She'd call me useless and I'd get pissed off. And in the end, she'd be heading home with the support she needed to recover, and I'd arrive in New York in plenty of time for my book tour.

But so far, nothing has gone as planned.

There is no time for further contemplation as I reach the doorway. A jolt of shock stops me in my tracks. I barely remember my grandmother. She died when I was little, but if my faulty memory serves me correct, the woman in the bed looks just like her.

Her hair is fully white. A few inches long, it spikes around her face like a thick lion's mane. Deep lines are carved around her eyes and into her cheeks, and her once granite jawline has softened. The formidable woman of my youth is gone, leaving behind this fragile husk.

The sight of her is disconcerting. How is it possible that she's changed so much? I've grown up, but she's grown old.

She looks helpless. Broken. In a flash, I regret every mean thing I've ever said about her. I hope she wakes up soon.

5

Half an hour passes with no change before I leave her bedside and head down the street to the police station. Stephen mentioned a Chief Sharpe, and if someone did attack my mother, I should know why.

The gal manning the front desk looks up as I enter. I brace myself for a frosty New York stare, but this gal's smile is friendly. Perky even. Slim, in her mid-twenties, she's wearing round glasses and a matching petal-pink sweater set.

"I'm here to see Chief Sharpe," I say.

"Do you have an appointment?"

"Could you tell him that Austin Martell is here?"

It's not the answer she's expecting, but the moment I see recognition dawning on her face, I am reminded that celebrity has its perks. She has heard of me. Maybe she's even read one of my books.

"The author?"

I nod. "And you are?"

"Anne Marie Baxter."

"Good to meet you, Anne Marie."

I shake her hand. She places her palms against her cheeks, which have turned as pink as her sweater.

"I'm afraid she's in a meeting right now."

"I can wait."

"I'm not sure how long she will be."

"It's okay," I assure her. "I've got time."

And I do. I suppose. Aside from the pages Diana has requested, I'm not chasing a book deadline or scheduled to attend a publicity event. I sit.

Minutes tick by. Waiting sucks. And this chair should come with a chiropractic warning. For all my bravado about having time to waste, I start to twitch. I'm tugging, twisting, and scratching at my beard. It's a bad habit, I know, and one I need to break, but for now...

I'm about to give up and text Rob when an office door near the back of the squad room opens. Anne Marie cocks her head.

"I'll be right back," she says.

True to her word, she returns a few moments later. I'm expecting her to tell me that I might as well head home. Instead, she leads me behind a locked barrier that separates the waiting area from the rest of the office without being frisked. The lack of a metal detector surprises me. I am ushered back toward the corner office with a lack of formality that I can barely comprehend is possible, let alone safe.

But maybe that's my New York sensibilities talking. Besides cow-tipping and petty theft, the island isn't exactly a hotbed of crime.

"Chief Sharpe, this is Austin Martell."

I glance over Anne Marie's shoulder. An electric jolt runs through me as I catch sight of the person seated behind the desk.

She looks different in uniform, but I would recognize those brown eyes anywhere. She looks just as surprised to see me standing in her doorway.

"Thank you, Anne Marie." She dismisses the young woman. A small smile plays at the corner of Ellie's mouth. "You can't possibly have had another emergency so soon."

"Wait, you're the chief of police?"

It's a dumb question, I know, but dammit, how is it possible that the pretty woman I met on the ferry is the same one I find sitting here? First off, she's a woman. I know how that sounds, but the

Whidbey Island I remember wasn't known for being progressive. I latch onto my second thought, hoping it sounds at least somewhat less chauvinistic.

"You're so young."

"And a woman," she says with a knowing smile, as if she can read my inner thoughts. "Funny, I've never heard that before."

Now it's my turn to blush. I'm not a misogynistic asshole. I'm not a misogynist anyway. The jury may still be out on the whole asshole part.

"Sorry. I just wasn't expecting to see you again so soon."

It's lame, and we both know it. The sight of her has knocked me sideways, and I'm trying to recover without looking like a total ass.

"Maybe we should start over."

She nods at my suggestion and gestures toward a chair. I take a seat.

"I was just at the hospital and—"

"You're Linda Martell's son," she interrupts.

"Austin, right."

"We've left messages."

"My phone died while I was in transit."

"That would explain it," she says.

"I was at the hospital today and Stephen...Doctor Alder advised me to come see you. He said that my mother's injuries may not have been the result of an accidental fall, and that you'd be able to fill me in on the investigation."

Ellie, I mean Chief Sharpe, nods.

"That's right. When Doctor Alder notified me, I dispatched a couple of officers to the scene. Unfortunately, they didn't uncover much evidence. No signs of forced entry or fingerprints."

My experience researching mysteries tells me that just because there's no definitive evidence proving a theory doesn't make it untrue.

"My mother used to keep a spare key in a basket of clothespins on the back porch."

Ellie cocks her head. "Was that common knowledge?"

I shrug. I knew it. So did Scott and all his friends who streamed in and out of the house during the long summers of our childhood. I have no idea who else she might have shared that information with. I don't even know for a fact that the key is still there, although I suspect that my mother, like most people of her generation, is a creature of habit.

"We'll check that out," she says and scribbles on a notepad. "Is there anyone you can think of that might have wanted to hurt your mother? Had she mentioned anything?"

"Truth is, we're not all that close."

I feel a stab of guilt at the admission. There's no hiding the fact that I've been a lousy son. Ellie watches the play of emotions ripple across my face with a curious expression of her own.

"Families can be complicated," she says, like she understands what I'm going through.

But how can she when I don't understand it myself? Scott could do no wrong, but she never passed up an opportunity to criticize me.

I thought I was over it—over her. But now, the complex rush of emotions I feel overwhelms me. I avert my gaze, keenly aware that Ellie is watching.

"You must have talked to the neighbors," I say.

"We did, but no one saw anything, or heard anything. Our current theory is that your mother was the victim of a break-in."

"But you said there was no evidence of forced entry."

Ellie shrugs. "There are still people on the island who don't lock their doors."

As a city-dweller, this concept seems foreign to me, although out here, it could well be true. My mother may have felt safe enough that she didn't lock her doors. Or she could have forgotten. Or maybe the thief discovered the hidden key. There are so many explanations. Too many. If my mother was awake, perhaps she could tell us what really happened.

"Will you be staying at her house, Austin?"

The casual use of my first name shakes me out of my stupor, and I grin.

"Unless there's a Ritz Carlton in town..."

"I'm afraid the island hasn't changed that much."

"Dare to dream," I sigh.

Ellie plucks a business card from a stack beside the monitor and hands it to me. For a brief second, our fingers touch. I feel a slight zing at the contact. Nothing in her expression tells me that she felt it too.

"In case of emergency," I say as I tuck the card into my pocket. She smiles at the inside joke. "Thanks for your time, Chief Sharpe."

The deliberate use of her title is a tease, and I can see she gets it. She promises to call me if she learns anything new and we shake hands like business acquaintances. For the next few seconds, we're both silent, and I realize that I'm staring. I want to look away, but the power of her gaze holds me in thrall. It's only when she breaks eye contact that I can breathe again.

On my way out of the office, I am left to contemplate the disturbing effect she has had on me in the brief time since we met.

6

I text the number Rob gave me, and within a minute or two, he pulls up in front of the police station. I open the passenger's door, and he hands me a coffee cup and a paper bag.

"You looked like you needed this."

Earthy steam wafts off the bitter Americano. The flakiest croissant known to man is inside the bag. My mouth waters as I tear off a bite. It's warm, and buttery, and amazing. My eyes roll back in my head.

"God, this is good. Thank you."

"My wife owns the bakery."

"Clearly you don't deserve her."

Rob laughingly agrees. I'm getting crumbs all over myself and the car, but I don't care. I didn't realize how hungry I was. I waste no time devouring the croissant. I wash the last of it down with the steaming black brew.

"Do you remember Cameron Pruitt?" Rob asks.

It takes a second, then I do. If Einstein and the Unabomber had a love child, it would have been Cameron.

"Wasn't he voted the most likely to colonize Mars? What's he up to?"

"Living out in the boonies." Rob grins. "I ran into him a few days ago. We were at Flyers, half cut, and he mentioned something that reminded me of you."

Flyers is the local watering hole for the military personnel based in Oak Harbor.

"Don't tell me he's read my books."

"Probably. He's always reading some damned thing. He was out diving with a few of his buddies and they came upon your brother's boat."

I freeze. I have no choice but to deal with the fallout from my mother's accident, but this? This is one part of my past that is not open for discussion. I hold up a hand.

"It doesn't matter. Scott's dead."

"I know, but he said there was something about the wreck that doesn't make sense."

"Stop!"

I didn't mean to snap, but Christ. An awkward silence falls between us as Rob focuses on the road. There's no need to give him directions. He remembers where I live. Rob pulls off the main highway and onto the twisty, tree-lined backroad leading to my mother's house.

I cringe as I catch sight of the one-story Cape Cod that has seen better days. A gentle breeze fans the waist-high grass waving across the lawn. The hulking hydrangea crowding the bay window looks as if it's being mugged by an overgrown blackberry bush.

Oh, hell no. I haven't done yardwork since college. Mowing the lawn is one thing, but taming this disaster is quite another. I'm already formulating excuses for not breaking out the hedge clippers when another thought strikes me.

How much worse is it inside?

"Ah, there's no place like home," Rob says.

Home. What a joke.

Rob gets out of the car and pops the trunk. He hauls out my suitcase and sets it down.

"If you find yourself at loose ends, stop by the Willows for a beer."

"Will do."

We shake hands, and seconds later, he's gone. I'm left here. Alone.

Creeping Charlie fans across the dusty driveway like furry spider webs and my suitcase rattles over the stones. I grab hold of the door handle and twist. The knob comes off in my hand. I laugh. With a sinking feeling, I know that Mom has let more than the yardwork slide.

I fumble around inside the basket of clothespins in search of the key. Finding it, I shove it into the lock. The damned thing sticks. I'm about to kick the door in when I remember the trick. I jiggle the key and wiggle the doorknob. It takes a good thirty seconds before it pops open with a click.

The deep silence inside the kitchen is unsettling. Mom hasn't made a single update I can see in the past fifteen years. No dishwasher. No microwave. And god have mercy on my soul, there's no electric coffee maker.

I groan. I can live without the other bits of modernization, but how in the name of all that is good and holy am I supposed to survive without coffee?

My mother's house is a shit heap. The kitchen table is piled high with a mountain of unopened mail the size of Mount Rainer. Everywhere I look, there's more stuff—boxes, books, magazines, newspapers, yarn, knitting needles, half-finished sweaters.

Gobsmacked, I walk through the rooms like an accident victim. I understand that some people aren't fastidious but...

"Jesus, Mom, when did you become a hoarder?" I mutter.

She's not here to answer, which makes what happens next even creepier.

I hear a noise. From down the hall. My heart jolts.

Every noise feels twice as loud in the preternatural silence. The hair prickles on the back of my neck. I hold my breath and hear a slight rustle of movement coming from the back of the house.

I look around for something to grab, you know, just in case there really is an intruder. I seize a frying pan off the stove. Clutching the handle, I head down the hallway. The ancient floors creak with every step.

Scott's bedroom is on the left. I pause outside his door and listen. *Nothing.* I keep going. The door to my old room is on the right. I grasp the handle.

But then I hear another noise. My heart booms.

It's coming from my mother's bedroom.

I tiptoe to the end of the hall and pause outside the door. It's dark in there. The blinds are drawn. I peek through the crack, looking for any sign of movement. It's so dark. I can't see a damned thing. I raise the frying pan and ease the door open.

A sudden flurry of footsteps erupts. I hear a loud hiss.

"What the—?" I yell, reeling back.

I slam into the wall as a gray cat skims by my legs. The frying pan clatters to the floor. The cat lets out a war cry as it jets down the hall.

A strangled laugh escapes me. I plant my hands on my knees, trying to catch my stupid breath. Some tough guy I am. Afraid of a stupid cat.

I return to the kitchen and toss the frying pan on the stove. Looking beyond the garbage and clutter I see thick rust-colored stains smeared across the floor. It's my mother's blood. The sight of it sickens me and I can't help thinking about my mother sprawled out here on the floor, hurt. Bleeding. Alone.

Stashed beneath the kitchen sink, I find a bucket and fill it with hot, soapy water. On hands and knees, I scrub the blood away. The water turns a darker shade of muddy brown as I wash the remainder of the floor.

I blow out a breath and rise.

It had to be a break-and-enter. What other motive would someone have to attack my mother? It's not like she has anything of value. Even if she did, how would anyone find it in this mess?

The thought depresses me. I dump the dirty water down the sink and rinse the bucket out. I should talk to her neighbors, her friends— try to figure out what happened, but not now. My eyes itch from all the dust. I need a shower. The wheels of my suitcase squeal across the still-damp floor as I tug it down the hall toward my old bedroom.

Christ.

If I thought the rest of the house was bad, it's nothing compared to my room. A hard nub of resentment forms in my heart as I stare at the mess. It's as if she opened the door and just pitched stuff inside, like she's burying any reminders of me beneath the layers of accumulated crap.

There's no way I can sleep in here.

I strip off my clothes in the middle of the hallway and head to the shower.

There's nothing wrong with the hot water tank. The spray from the showerhead scalds me. I yelp and crank the dial back. The water cools, and I angle my face up into the spray.

This is the most human I've felt in over twenty-four hours. I emerge from the shower feeling revived.

God, I'm starving. I knot a towel around my waist and go in search of food. The refrigerator's motor rumbles as loud as a freaking transport when I open the door to take stock of the shelves. There's nothing edible in here. Besides condiments and leftovers, which are already sprouting mold, there's blessed little in the fridge. There's even less inside the cupboards.

Are you kidding me? I will not eat pea soup from a can. I was forced to eat this stuff growing up and I swear that I would rather starve first. And if the rumble of my tummy is any indication, I might be halfway there. Behind the stacked tins of Fancy Feast, I find a jar of peanut butter and a half-eaten sleeve of saltines and haul it out.

I twist the lid off and grimace. There is an inch of oil sitting on top of the peanut butter. I forgot how much my mother loves this stuff. Real peanut butter, she calls it. I call it disgusting, but hey, it beats pea soup or death.

I search the drawers for a butter knife and plunge it into the thick clay depths. It's like mixing concrete. I clench my teeth and continue to stir until the oil splashes over the edge and spills onto the freshly washed floor.

Dammit.

I spread a thick layer of gooey stuff onto a cracker and shove it into my mouth. Even prisoners eat better than this, I swear. There's no salt in the peanut butter and the cracker's stale. Still, I force myself to choke down a few more.

Now that I'm no longer in danger of dying, I retrieve my laptop bag and head into the living room. Navigating my mother's house is like walking through a maze. There's a narrow path of exposed carpet carved out between the piles of crap. One of those paths leads me to the couch. I collapse onto the worn cushions. The couch groans, as if I've offended it. Seriously, it has nothing to complain about. The last time I sat here, I was a much heavier guy.

I dismiss the thought and open the laptop. The display springs to life at the push of a button, filling me with giddy relief.

This I know. This is the one thing here that's mine.

Within seconds, I've launched the word processor and the black cursor blinks merrily on the blank page. My fingers caress the keys and I wait for a thought to strike me.

The opening line doesn't need to be perfect, it just needs to...

My fingers tap lightly on the keys, but nothing comes to mind.

Come on.

I can do this. I've always been able to do this—forget everything else and fall into the black hole, allowing the words to flow from my fingers onto the page, as if someone else is writing them.

But half an hour later, the page is still blank. The cursor throbs on the screen, mocking me, and I snap the lid shut. What is wrong with me? It's the house... I can't think here. It's too crowded. Too dark. Too...

I can't even finish the thought. I've got to get out of here. It's 10:30 New York time and there's still plenty of light in the sky. Maybe after some fresh air, and some real food, I'll be ready to write.

The thought cheers me. I abandon my laptop and dig through my suitcase for some clean clothes. I pull on my favorite jeans and a plum-colored T-shirt. The soft, buttery feel of the leather loafers against my bare toes makes me smile, and I go in search of the car keys.

Thank god I don't have to search far. They're hanging on a hook beside the kitchen door. While my mother would score an F in safety, she gets an A in predictability. Right now, I'm not inclined to quibble. The kitchen door slams shut as I stride into the garage. The smell of dust and motor oil hits me as I fumble for the lights. I try not to think of what kind of motorized abomination is hiding in here. It's probably a rusty Chevy, or worse, a Dodge Dart.

The lights flick on and I gasp in shock at what I find.

How is it possible that I've forgotten about the Mustang convertible my father left behind? As far back as I can recall, the car sat hidden beneath a dusty tarp. But now...it's been fully restored. It's as if the automotive fairy waved a magic wand and voila. I blink in disbelief as I descend the stairs and walk toward it.

It's jaw-droppingly gorgeous. The exterior is painted a deep cherry red. The seats are as soft as silk, and I run my hands across the leather. The engine starts on the first try, filling the garage with its full-throated growl.

Okay, I'm a little out of practice. It takes two tries to get it into reverse. But once I'm clear of the driveway, it's smooth sailing. The evening is warm. I leave the top down as I cruise down the backroads toward civilization. The gentle wind ruffling my hair smells of saltwater and cedar. Up ahead, I see the turn-off for town.

The actual town hasn't grown much in the years since I left, but what is here is a blend of the old and the new. The general store is still in the middle of Main Street, with its bipolar mix of groceries, housewares, and clothes. There's a café on the right, along with a small bookstore. High-end tourist shops line the left side, inhabiting the space where the local Salvation Army store used to be. Baskets of cascading flowers hang from the lampposts, giving the town a postcard-like feel.

At the top of the hill, I see the resort. The Willows.

Getting out of the house was a good idea. A drink or two and something to eat might be exactly the thing I need to kick-start my muse. I park next to a white Karmann Ghia convertible. The sweet scent of honeysuckle greets me as I climb the stairs to the wide oak door. The bell rings overhead.

The Willows' lobby is clean and welcoming. Brown leather furniture is gathered around the river rock fireplace, giving the place a warm, inviting feel. Soft music mingles with the sound of laughter drifting from the dining room. Beyond the dining room is a darker nook—the bar. I turn in that direction when I catch sight of her.

Her hair is the color of winter wheat. It falls past her shoulders in a sleek curtain that catches the light. She's talking to the woman beside her when her eyes lift and collide with mine. Cornflower blue, they pop wide. The color drains from her face.

A water glass slides from her hand. In a crash, it shatters on the floor.

7

I rush in to pick up the shards of glass. Her cheeks blush a deep fuchsia. She doesn't look at me as she piles broken glass onto a tray. Finally, the mess is cleared away and the floor swept clean as we straighten.

"I'll take this," the woman beside Leigh says as she departs, leaving her with no choice but to look at me then.

"Austin," she says, pressing her palms to her burning cheeks.

I spy an emerald cut diamond ring and a white gold wedding band. The ring must go with the baby bump expanding her belly.

"It's good to see you, Leigh."

I almost tell her that she looks as beautiful as ever, but the line sounds trite. She smiles and gives a nervous laugh.

"I'm not usually such a klutz, it's just such a shock seeing you. You've grown a beard."

I scratch self-consciously at the neatly trimmed beard. Instinctively, I know why the sight of me startled her, though neither of us wants to say. It's the reason why I grew the beard in the first place. Without it, I look disturbingly like my brother, Scott.

"And look at you," I say, deflecting the awkwardness of the moment. "You've grown a baby."

She laughs and spreads a hand across her belly.

"Why, yes, I'm working on it. When did you get home?"

There's that word again. *Home.* It's such a loaded term, not only used to describe the place where you live, but it is rife with overtones of family, of belonging, of being somewhere with people who love you. Did I ever feel that way? I'm not sure. If I had, it was so long ago that I don't remember it.

"Today."

"I heard about your mom. How is she?"

"Ah, you know what they say. Only the good die young, which means she'll live forever."

"Austin!" Despite the shocked look on her face, she laughs, and I grin.

"She'll recover," I say, making light of the situation, because it's easier, because there are some places I'd rather not go.

"It's good of you to come. Let me buy you a drink."

"Now that's the best offer I've had since I left Manhattan."

She leads the way across the lobby toward the bar. I follow, admiring the décor.

"I love what you've done with the place."

"Thanks," she says. "I took it over about five years ago."

"From your parents?"

Leigh nods. "They retired, moved to Phoenix. Said they couldn't stand the rain another second."

"I can appreciate that."

For eight months of the year, living in the Pacific Northwest is kind of like living inside of a car wash.

I climb onto a nearby stool and take in my surroundings. The bar has an urban, rustic feel all the rage now in New York, where restaurant and bar owners pay a fortune for old, weathered barn boards while the farmers are laughing their assess off all the way to the bank. High wood-topped tables are adorned with clear glass lanterns. Soft music fills the place.

The waitress spots Leigh the moment we walk in and beelines it toward our table.

"What can I get the two of you?"

Leigh orders a cranberry and soda. They both look at me.

I love martinis more than life. Okay, that's a slight exaggeration. And looking around I know I should probably play it safe and order a glass of wine. Assuming it's not box-au-vin, you can't really screw things up. Instead, I blurt the first thing out that comes to mind.

"A vodka martini. Dry and dirty. On the rocks."

Please, god, don't let it suck, I think to myself. This day's already been trying enough.

"I remember when you used to sneak sips from my wine coolers," Leigh says.

"I remember when you used to have freckles on your nose."

She smiles. Scarfing down a handful of pretzels from the clear glass bowl on the table, I hear the ghost of my mother's voice say, *Stop now before you eat the whole thing, piggy.*

I push the bowl away.

"So, married, a baby on the way, and a successful business. Your first?"

"Business, husband, or baby?" she asks.

"I was thinking baby, but feel free to touch on any that apply."

Her smile fades and I realize I've unwittingly stepped on a landmine.

"I've had some trouble in the baby department."

"I'm sorry. I hope everything goes smoothly this time. Husbands?" I ask.

"Still on my first. And you?"

"No husbands."

"Funny," she quips.

"And business? Looks good from where I'm sitting."

Two thirds of the tables are full, and I hear the happy buzz of chatter all around.

"It's Labor Day weekend, and holiday weekends are always good for business. I won't lie. The downturn in the economy has taken its toll. Fewer people travelling. I've been advertising weekend getaway packages priced to entice Seattleites to leave America and come to the island."

America? Oh yeah. I'd forgotten the island slang.

"And though we're seeing an uptick in reservations, it isn't a direct translation to bottom line. I don't understand why."

"You're not in trouble, are you?"

"Not yet, but if things don't turn around soon, we might be."

It's on the tip of my tongue to say *that's business for ya*, because it's what I would say to one of my New York friends. But this is Leigh. When I was a chubby high school nerd, Leigh was good to me. And when she touches her tummy, it's such a nurturing and maternal gesture that I can't help it. I melt.

"I met a guy when I was researching a book. He's a forensic accountant—a genius with numbers. If anyone can pinpoint what's going wrong with your business, it would be him. I could ask him for a favor if you think it would help."

Her face brightens. "You'd do that?"

"Consider it done."

The waitress stops by with our drinks. I know it makes me a snob to say this, but it's a better martini than I expected, delicious and briny. I take another sip. The icy vodka slides down my throat and I can feel my shoulders relax. Turns out that after the hellish day I've endured, a drink is just what the doctor ordered. I'm about to say as much when a tall man approaches.

Okay, I wouldn't admit this to everyone, but he has the kind of build I've always envied, with thickly muscled shoulders and C-cup pecks, narrowing away to what I'm sure amounts to six-pack abs.

I'm in good shape. I run twenty miles a week, do yoga and Pilates, but I've never been much into weight training. So, while my build remains trim and toned, it lacks his sheer size and power.

He barely glances in my direction, as his attention rests solely on Leigh. By the way she smiles at him, I know this must be the husband.

I pick up the menu and peruse the items while they exchange a kiss.

"Honey, why don't you go home and get some rest? I can take care of things from here."

"Soon," she answers, reaching across the table and touching my wrist. "Blake, you remember Austin."

I glance up and take in his face. A jolt of surprise shoots through me so strong that it's like I've just grabbed hold of an electric wire with my bare hands and can't let go. He's more than familiar. *I know him.* He looks equally shocked to see me. A couple beats of silence pass.

"Of course," he says with a faltering smile, like he just remembered his manners.

He offers his hand and we shake like old acquaintances. Only that's an understatement. If Leigh was a frequent visitor to my childhood home, Blake Parsons practically lived there. He was my brother's best friend from as far back as I can remember. I haven't seen him since the day of the storm when he and Scott climbed aboard the sailboat. Blake was the only one who made it back.

"What brings you home?" he asks. The polite question sounds forced. I can see the sight of me unsettles him.

"Mom had an accident."

He nods without passing comment. His arm circles around Leigh and he gathers her close to his side. The gesture seems so casual, so natural, that Leigh doesn't seem to notice that she's being branded. But I do.

"Sorry to hear that. How long will you be staying?"

"A few weeks."

His lips curl into a ghost of a smile, but his eyes lack Leigh's warmth.

"Well, it's good to see you, Austin. I don't know if she mentioned it, but Leigh here's a big fan. She's got all your books."

Leigh blushes prettily. "He's right. I've been following your career. You're a celebrity around here—local boy does good."

"Thank you," I say looking modestly away.

"I'd love it if you'd sign my books sometime. If it's not an imposition."

"For you? Anything."

Her eyes widen slightly, as if a sudden thought occurs to her, and she glances up at Blake.

"You know, we're having the auction tomorrow night."

"Easy, Leigh," Blake says.

"What kind of auction?"

The moment the words slip out, I want to take them back. I hate auctions. Besides, I have no desire to rub elbows with the locals. I already see ghosts from my past everywhere I turn. And hell, I've got a book to write.

"It's a fundraiser for the hospital. I'd love it if we could auction off a set of autographed books."

I'm relieved. It's a simple request and signing books happens to be one of my favorite things to do.

"Of course, I'll stop by tomorrow afternoon."

"Great, I'll pick them up from the bookstore tomorrow morning and leave them at the front desk. Only..."

Uh-oh. I can tell the other shoe is about to drop.

"Only?"

"Well, if you were here..."

"Honey," Blake says, tightening his grip on her shoulders. "I'm sure Austin has more important things to do than attend the auction. He's got his mother to worry about. Besides, a big New York celebrity like him would find our little shindig boring."

The condescending way he says this makes my hackles rise. And what's worse, Leigh's face falls like a kid who's just been told there's no Santa Claus. She nods.

"You're right. I wasn't thinking."

"I would be delighted to join you," I hear myself say.

I would rather have my toenails ripped out with a pair of rusty plyers, but whatever pain this might cause me is totally worth it when I see Blake's smug smile wilt.

"You will? Oh my god, Austin, that would be amazing."

Blake was always kind of a dick. When he was with Scott, I may as well have not existed, unless they wanted me to grab some contraband from the kitchen—chips, snacks, the last soda. They would raid the fridge after practice, then I'd be the one who got blamed. And after Scott died, Blake never came by the house. Not once.

Everyone made excuses for him, but the truth was that the only person Blake cared about was himself. How Leigh ended up with an asshole like him, I will never know.

And then, as if I'm being rewarded for my magnanimous gesture, a fresh martini arrives. I thank the waitress and order a cobb salad before she has the chance to disappear. I promise Leigh that I will arrive on time for the gala dinner.

"Seriously, Austin, you're the best."

She grabs my hand and gives it a squeeze.

"No problem."

When I see the gorgeous woman approaching our table, I almost choke on my martini. She is sex in a dress. With a flirty smile, she catches my eye, and Leigh turns toward the newcomer.

"Carley," Leigh says.

I'm surprised I don't get frostbite from the chill in Leigh's voice. She casts a sidelong glance at Blake, but his expression is more tightly shuttered than a vacation rental in storm season. Leigh wiggles off the bar stool and wedges a hand in the small of her back.

"You know, honey, I am tired. It's time to go."

"I hope it's nothing I said," I joke.

Leigh doesn't answer. She brushes a kiss across my cheek and whispers, "I'm so glad you're home."

Blake rests his hand on Leigh's back and guides her toward the exit. He shoots me a stony look from the doorway before they depart.

"Austin Martell!" the woman exclaims. "I can't believe you're here. The last time I saw you was at a book signing in New York, though you probably don't remember. There were so many people. I'm Carley Darling... It used to be Carley Braun, but you know..."

"You do look familiar."

She gives a husky laugh and favors me with a flirty upturned glance. "I'll bet you say that to all the girls. Mind if I join you?"

I wave my hand toward the stool Leigh has just vacated and she slides in across from me. Pushing a strand of chestnut hair out of her face, she fixes me with an ultra-bright smile. The blinding flash of perfect teeth reminds me of the Starbucks barista from the airport this morning. There must be a Groupon for Crest White Strips on the West Coast.

"I used to be friends with your brother, but then you probably don't remember that either."

Unlike Bruce Springsteen, and at least half of the citizens inhabiting the island, my glory days were not in high school. I've done my best to eradicate those memories from my mind, but I do remember something about Carley.

"You were a cheerleader, right?"

"Right you are." Her smile is positively incandescent. "And you... you're such an awesome writer. I've read all your books."

"Thanks. That's kind of you to say."

"So, tell me, what has lured you from the bright city lights to our sleepy little neck of the woods?"

"Mom had an accident."

"That's right. I heard. How is she?"

Of course she's heard. Everyone's heard. I shrug.

"Stable. Would you like to join me for a drink?"

"Are you kidding?"

She smiles again. She glances down at the wine list while I study her face in the flickering candlelight. The years have been good to her. She is as gorgeous now as she was back then, and I wonder how many freckles she has hiding underneath that amazing dress. I'm admiring the lovely curve of her cleavage when she looks up suddenly, catching my gaze.

I know I should be embarrassed, but I'm not. I stare directly into her wide green eyes.

"What are you drinking?" she asks.

"A vodka martini."

"Oh, you're hardcore." She folds a hand under her chin and smiles. "I'm more of a lightweight. Fruity cocktails when it's sunny, wine all other times."

"I would have pegged you for a Budweiser girl."

She wrinkles her pert little nose. "Are you mistaking me for a redneck?"

"Well, if the town fits…"

"I get it. You're screwing with me," she says.

I grin, and she bats her eyelashes.

"Not yet."

Her mouth drops open. She's about to respond with something naughty when the waitress interrupts.

"What can I get you?"

Does Carley secrete some kind of pheromone that pisses other women off? The waitress is barely civil. It's all so disturbingly high school.

"Chardonnay, please," Carley says.

The waitress nods. She places the salad plate in front of me, and I can't help it, I could kiss her, the food looks so good.

"How is it, being home?"

I gesture toward my food in a wordless offer to share, but she shakes her head.

"Fine." I answer dutifully. I'm only going to be asked this a million times over the next few days. I pick up my fork and start to eat. "Tell me more about you."

"Oh, I need a drink for that." She glances toward the bar and fingers a dangly gold earring dripping from her earlobe.

"That bad?"

"Well, let's just say I've made some bad decisions."

"Bad decisions? Those make the best stories."

The waitress shows up on cue and sets the wine on the table. I pick up my martini and clink it against her glass.

"Here's to bad decisions."

"Amen." She laughs and takes a sip.

"So?" I prod.

"Where do you want to start?"

"College?"

"Evergreen State College."

"You mean the hippie school out in Olympia?"

I catch a flash of white teeth.

"That's the one." Chestnut curls dance delightfully around her face as she bobs her head. "I had some problems my final year."

"What kind of problems?"

She hesitates, and I incline my head and flash an apologetic smile.

"I'm pathologically nosy. All good authors are."

"Wait a minute. I'm not going to find my sob story on the pages of your next book, am I?"

"My books are works of fiction. Names, characters, businesses, places, and events are the products of my overactive imagination. Any resemblance to persons, living or dead, is purely coincidental. I swear."

"All right, then. Health problems."

She's holding something back, and I decide not to probe. I'm enjoying our flirty exchange too much to let reality spoil it.

"Nothing too awful, I hope."

She shrugs. It's another non-answer. I like her more already.

"I went to live with my mom for a while. Got married. He turned out to be a little crazy."

"And by crazy you mean...?"

"A stalker type."

"Oh dear, am I in any danger?"

"I guess that depends on your intentions."

"Well..." I say, as if I'm reluctant to divulge the truth.

"No need to worry. He's long gone."

"Whew. Good riddance. So, you're divorced?"

"Not exactly. I mean, not yet. With him gone, there didn't seem to be much need. Anyway, I got my real estate license, and now I'm working in Dad's business."

I drop my napkin on top of the empty plate and sip my martini.

"So, you sell houses?" I say.

"You in the market?"

"Me? Ha. I can barely afford my flat back in New York."

"Flat. That's very British."

"We writers have our quirks."

"Do tell." She cups her hand under her chin and leans forward. I feel the pull of her—sweet. Sexy.

"It's a long story."

"Those are the best kind," she says.

I'm about to say something witty when her cell phone rings. She glances at the screen.

"Do you need to get that?"

"Probably," she says, but makes no effort to answer the call.

Her gaze is locked with mine. I'm picking up on her pheromones now.

"What do you say we get out of here?"

"Are all New York girls easy?"

"The fun ones are."

She cocks her head and smiles.

"Well then, let's go."

8

I wake up in a strange place. It's dark. I feel the sharp jut of a shoulder digging into my back. It takes me a second to recall where I am. *Carley's.* We jumped in her white Karmann Ghia and left the Willows behind.

Carley owns a rancher outside Coupeville. She claims there's a peekaboo view of the beach, but it was so dark when we pulled in, I couldn't see a thing. And once we were inside...

Her arms locked around me. I felt every one of her delectable curves press against my chest. Together, we moved through the dark house—from the living room to the bedroom. Two shadows intertwined, and well...

In the quiet of the house, I hear her breathing—slow and steady. Gently, I peel her arm off me and place it on the bed. She murmurs but doesn't wake. Easing off the mattress, I retrieve my clothes from the floor. My shoes are by the door, and I pull them on.

I'm an idiot! Why didn't I insist on following her here in my car? Now I'm stuck here, unless...

The fact that Rob answers the text in a matter of seconds eases my conscience.

You weren't sleeping, were you?

Hell, no. Poker with the boyz. Want to join?

Got time to give me a ride?

Where?

It's a good question. It takes a few seconds to locate the address. I punch it in.

Be there soon.

I wait for Rob outside. It's early September, and though the days are warm, the nights are cooling off quickly. My arms are crossed and I'm shivering by the time Rob arrives. The headlights swing into the driveway and I cringe, hoping the blinding white shafts of light don't wake Carley.

I rush to the car and close the door as softly as I can. Thank god the heater is blasting. I can smell the rum on Rob's breath as he throws the gearshift into reverse.

"So?" Rob asks, rolling his curious gaze my way.

"So?"

"Don't play dumb. How was she?"

"A gentleman never kisses and tells."

"Yeah, a gentleman," Rob says with a laugh. "Where I'm from, a gentleman doesn't sneak out in the middle of the night."

"In Manhattan, it's considered impolite to be underfoot while someone gets ready for work."

"Ha! You're a long way from Manhattan."

"She knows this can't go anywhere."

"Does she?"

"Sure. Once Mom wakes up, I'll be homeward bound."

"If you say so, but let me give you a piece of advice that my eighth grade teacher once said to me," Rob says. He clears his throat and continues in a voice that is a cross between James Earl Jones and the cookie monster. "Rob, my boy, if you only remember one thing from our time together, remember this. Never sleep with a woman crazier than you."

"Really? I'm pretty sure we had the same eighth grade teacher, and I can guarantee you that if he said that, I would have remembered."

"Maybe you were sick that day."

I snicker and shake my head. Rob is driving a good fifteen miles over the speed limit, and despite the smell of rum on his breath, I'm not nervous. He knows these roads like the back of his hand. There's not another soul in sight.

"What is it about Carley? It's like everyone has a hate on for her."

"Did you know that her husband's missing?" Rob asks, shooting a gaze my way.

"Missing? You mean he left her."

"Is that what she told you?"

Between the martinis and the fact that it's nearly six in the morning New York time, I'm a little fuzzy on the details, but I sure as hell would have remembered a *missing* husband.

"Look. I appreciate the warning, but seriously, I'm going to be here a nanosecond. None of this matters."

"If you say so." He shrugs.

The two of us drive in silence back to the Willows. I tip him an indecent amount of money before climbing out of his car. It's after three when I park the Mustang in the driveway and stumble inside the house. I'm too bagged to do anything about my room, and there is no way I'm sleeping in my mother's bed. Ever. I can't bring myself to step foot into Scott's room, so the couch it is.

It's no big deal. A few nights on the couch won't kill me. I'm asleep within seconds.

A heron's scream, as shrill as a human in pain, pierces the thick cloud of sleep, and I jar awake, gasping like I've been held under the water too long. My eyes pop open. My heart stops. I'm not alone.

Jade green eyes, as cold as marbles, bore into me. Hot, rancid breath fills my nostrils. Leaning toward me, the intruder is so close, we're nose to nose.

I half yelp, half scream. Claws pierce my chest like tiny Ginsu knives. As quick as a snake, the cat leaps from my chest and is out of the living room so fast I can barely catch my breath. *Christ.* It's like a scene out of that Stephen King movie, *Sleepwalkers*, where cats suck the life force out of virgin women. But I'm not a woman, or a virgin, and now I can't remember whether the cats were the enemies or the heroes. Never mind. It doesn't matter.

There is something very wrong with that cat. My pulse roars in my ears, and I struggle to catch my breath. Then I move. *Oh, man.* My back shrieks—the muscles seize as tight as a rusty pump. Apparently, there are fewer than six degrees of separation between my mother's view of the ideal couch and a medieval torture device.

I groan as I push myself up and swing my legs over the side. My head booms and I feel like shit—jet lag, martinis, you name it, and I need a shower. I shed my boxer shorts and T-shirt on the floor and walk naked down the hallway toward the bathroom.

While I'd never do something so careless in my New York condo, it's barely noticeable in the wreck of my mother's house. I scratch my chest and feel something wet. I look down. Ruby beads of blood are smudged across my white skin. *Damned cat.*

I set the water temperature as cold as I can stand in the vain hope it will jolt me out of my stupor. In need of some Tylenol, I yank open the medicine cabinet. The ancient door rips free from the hinges and the knob breaks off in my hand. The door plummets from my grasp and the mirror shatters on the edge of the sink. Broken glass rains down in a million silver shards on the bathroom floor.

A large curved piece of glass slices through the skin on my forearm like a filet knife, leaving a red half-moon crescent-shaped cut. Other fragments open small fissures in my hand and knuckles.

Dammit.

I'm bleeding, and it burns. I run my arm under the cool water and hiss. The good news is that none of the cuts look very deep. I wrap a ratty towel around my arm and pick my way through the glass.

I should head to the hospital and check in on Mom. I need to talk to Stephen about her condition—what he thinks is going to happen long term.

The long cut on my forearm is still oozing blood as I pass through the hospital's sliding doors. Mrs. Newman flags me down.

"Austin, I thought it might be good for you to talk with our home-care coordinator. Her name's Julie. Nice lady. I'll let her know you're here. She's meeting with another family now, but I'm sure she can stop by your mother's room afterwards."

A prickle of irritation creeps up my spine. One of the things I've always hated about small towns is that everyone knows everyone else's business.

"I'm sorry. I didn't mean to overstep," she says, as if reading my thoughts.

"No, Mrs. Newman. It's good. Thank you. I was just surprised. That's all."

On my way down the hall, I pass a nurse dressed in green scrubs. She eyes my improvised field dressing with disdain. She doesn't return my grin and I forget all about her as I see Stephen leaving Mom's room.

"Is she awake?" I ask.

Stephen shakes his head. "Not yet. There's been no change since yesterday."

"What are you thinking, longer term?"

Stephen raises his palm. "I wish I could tell you, but it's too soon to know for sure."

The answer is along the lines of what I expected, but still... "Are we talking days? Weeks? Longer?"

"We need to take it one day at a time, Austin. I hear you're meeting with homecare."

Seriously? Gossip spreads faster than the flu around here.

"So Mrs. Newman tells me."

Stephen nods. I'm about to say that if we don't know what kind of care Mom is going to need, what's the point, but just then he catches sight of the hobo field dressing.

"Jesus, Austin, what did you do?"

"The house is trying to kill me. This morning it sent the bathroom mirror to do its bidding."

"Looks like it won," he says with a smirk.

Taking hold of my wrist, he peeks beneath the blood-stained rag.

"It's just a flesh wound," I joke, but Stephen looks unamused.

"I'll send a nurse by to clean out your cuts. You may need stitches."

"I've survived literary reviews that cut more deeply than this."

"When was the last time you had a tetanus shot?"

"Look, if I need last rites, I'll give you a call. Otherwise..."

"Don't tell me you're still a baby about needles."

Stephen was with me the day I passed out donating blood.

"It wasn't the needle, it was the way she wielded it like a dagger that got me. I mean, really, she would have made a better butcher than a nurse."

"Whatever. Remember you said that when you show up next week with an infection or, worse, lockjaw."

"You could be so lucky," I snipe.

His laughter carries down the hallway as I turn into my mother's room. Not a damned thing has changed since I saw her yesterday, and yet the weight of dread presses down on my chest at the sight of her immobile form. Another son might take his mother's hand and tell her that everything will be all right, but as much as I know I should, I can't bring myself to do it.

I still remember what she said to me the morning of Scott's funeral. Some things are too painful to forget.

"Mr. Martell?"

I turn away from the bed as the homecare coordinator enters the room. I have no doubt the woman behind me was a knockout in her day. She's over fifty with red hair, blue eyes, and a pretty smile. She holds out her hand and we shake.

"I'm Julie Martin. Sorry I'm late."

"No problem."

She releases my hand, but her gaze lingers on my arm.

"Are you having that looked at?"

"It's nothing."

She cocks her head as though she doesn't quite believe me, but unlike Stephen, she lets it drop.

"Would you like to talk in here?"

She motions toward the two chairs at the foot of the hospital bed.

Frankly, I would rather be sitting on a bucket platform poised above a dunk tank filled with piranhas than in this hospital room.

"I'm sorry about your mom's accident. This can't be easy for you."

I have no desire to delve into the complex morass of emotions churning beneath the surface. Contrary to what my shrink might say, denial works for me.

"Aside from the fact that there isn't a single grain of coffee in the house, and my mother's cat is plotting my demise, I'd say I'm holding up remarkably well. Thank you."

She laughs softly at my deflection.

"We can't know exactly what your mother will need— "

"Until she wakes up," I interrupt, channeling Stephen.

"Right. But we do know that patients with traumatic brain injury sometimes suffer from memory loss or physical impairments. She'll likely move from here to a rehab facility. From there, it will depend on her progress. Whether she can stand, walk, care for herself..." Julie trails off.

I'm fiddling with the edge of the makeshift dressing, avoiding her gaze. She pauses, as if she's trying to gage my reaction. My expression gives nothing away. Julie continues.

"You may want to consider visiting some assisted living facilities while you're on the island, in case she needs more support. Especially since you live so far away."

I pull in a quick breath at the jab of pain that strikes at the mention of a nursing home. These are the kinds of grown-up decisions I never envisioned having to make. I'm not ready to face them yet.

Julie touches my injured arm in a comforting gesture. I straighten and ease away.

"I know. It's a lot to take in. We don't have to make any decisions today." Julie lingers for a few minutes more, then leaves me alone with my thoughts. I never expected to be left in charge of my mother's care. How should I know what she wants? It's a terrible thing to contemplate. So I don't. I exit the hospital through the emergency room doors. No sooner do I pull into my mother's driveway than my phone goes off.

Jaws.

I dismiss the call. It's not even lunchtime and I've already dealt with enough shit today. I send the call straight to voicemail and go in search of some food. I choke down the godawful peanut butter straight from the jar. Not wanting to be responsible for killing the cat, I open a tin of Fancy Feast.

If the cat is in this house, it's nowhere to be found. I set the can on the floor along with a small bowl of water.

The floor squeals in protest as I make my way down the hall. I slow as I walk toward Scott's room. I stop outside his door. Reach for the door handle. It has been years since I allowed myself to think about Scott, but now I miss him with a visceral ache. Losing a brother is like losing a part of yourself. Sure, we fought. Sure, I got tired of living in his shadow. But he stuck up for me. When I needed him, he was there, and now...

I wish he was here. He would know what to do about Mom. He was always better at handling her than I was.

I turn the knob and open the door a crack and stop. I can't go in there. The only thing awaiting me inside is more pain. I close the door and head to the living room.

My laptop is sitting on the floor. With a sigh, I flop down on the couch and power it on. What I wouldn't give to lose myself in a story right now. Something I can control. Something to make me forget. I close my eyes and will it to come—a line, a character, a place. Anything.

But nothing. Not a goddamned thing comes to mind. Normally, I would search the internet for inspiration, or catch up on social media while my subconscious spins. But not here. Here I am on an internet-starved desert island surrounded by password-protected Wi-Fi islands that mock me.

I spend a full hour in front of a blank screen before giving up. I slam the lid closed.

I sigh. It's no use. I can't focus. I've got too much shit whirling around inside my mind. At least I can do one thing...

I pull out my cell phone and search through my emails until I find the number for my forensic accountant friend. By the fifth ring, I'm rehearsing a message in my head when he picks up.

"Craig, this is Austin Martell."

A beat of silence passes.

"Austin, hi. This is a nice surprise. What's up?"

"Look, I've got this friend—she owns a resort on Whidbey Island. Long story short, she's having some cash flow problems. I was wondering if you could look at her books and see if you could figure out what's going on."

"Sure. Anything for my favorite author. It may take a few days to get to it though."

"No problem. Whenever you can fit it in. I know she'd appreciate the help."

I relay Leigh's contact information and hang up.

The heat of the house feels oppressive and I decide to go for a run. I never go anywhere without packing my running gear. Even if I don't use it, I still bring it with me. Like Linus from the Peanuts, it's my security blanket. Especially here, where I remember all too well how it feels to be chubby.

I pull on a pair of black running shorts and a bright Nike shirt and go digging for my shoes. All geared up, I emerge from the house into the afternoon sun. It's a glorious day and I stretch for a full two minutes before heading off at a jog.

West.

A gentle breeze ruffles the trees. The smell of the salt air beckons to me. The first mile is hard. The first mile is always hard, but as the rural road unfurls before me, my mind empties. This is my Zen.

My sneakers pound the asphalt and I hear the distant buzz of cars. Sunlight skims across the dark blue sea, and I head toward it—without thinking, without feeling. And before I know it, three miles have passed, and my custom-fit Nikes are crunching on the stony beach. I stop. My chest heaves. Sweat runs down my back. It takes me a second to realize where I am.

Deception Bay.

I didn't mean to come here. It is as if I was drawn here by some unforeseen force. A gust of wind blows off the water. I shudder. And as much as I want to turn away, I can't. Distant memories murmur like shells in the tide.

Somewhere out there, beyond the rocky point, my brother's boat went down. He never came home. The momentary thought of what Cameron might have seen invades my mind. The boat, cast on its side, still and silent beneath the murky waters of Puget Sound. And what else?

I remember the first year Scott was gone—how it felt like a part of me had died along with him.

I thought I'd moved on, but my brother is here, on this island, everywhere I look. And here, of all places, I can no longer pretend that he didn't exist. I want to go back to New York. I want everything to return to the way it was. But it won't. For better or worse, I'm stuck here, until my mother finally wakes up.

9

The run wasn't the silver bullet I was hoping for. The afternoon passed with no progress on the new story, and suddenly it's time to leave. When I arrive at the Willows, the parking lot is packed. I circle the lot looking for an open spot and finally wedge the Mustang into a dodgy corner overgrown with blackberry bushes. A branch snags me. The thorns bite into my flesh as I work to extricate myself from its grasp and head toward the front door.

The girl at the reception desk spots me the moment I enter the lobby. I pivot past a couple of tourists dressed in ball caps and cargo shorts on my way over.

"Mr. Martell, so glad you could make it tonight. Mrs. Parsons left these for you."

Mrs. Parsons? The reference stumps me for half a moment, until I realize she's talking about Leigh. The clerk places my four novels in a neat stack on the desk, ordering them from first to last. Smiling, she hands me a pen.

"I'm a big fan," she gushes.

I've been to book signings where the author looks like they would rather be shot dead than expose themselves to another fan, but I'm nowhere near that jaded. I enjoy this part of my job. Besides, there's a simple formula I follow to ensure success every time—look a person in the eye, make it personal, and sign your name.

Lather. Rinse. Repeat.

"Thank you." I smile graciously. "What's your name?"

"Karen. Karen Larson. I write a little too."

She gives me a shy look like she's imparting a secret. I pause, then open the first book to the title page.

"Wonderful. What do you write, Karen?"

"I'm ashamed to say...romances."

She blushes. I smile and pen an inscription in red ink. Closing the first book, I move on to the next.

"If I were you, I wouldn't be ashamed in the least. Romance sells more than any other genre."

"Really?" She beams, looking like I've just awarded her the Pulitzer.

I nod and gaze directly into her dancing eyes.

"Who doesn't want to read a story that engages your heart?"

She presses her fingers to her lips as I open the third book. I used to suck at signing books. You want to write something that's witty and memorable. Not as easy as it seems. I was so nervous at my first book signing that I barely looked up. Consequently, I ended up writing a flirty inscription meant for a girl to a guy wearing motorcycle boots and a flannel shirt. Definitely not my best moment.

"These will make a killing in the silent auction," Karen says as I hand over the fourth book.

"I hope so. Nice to meet you, Karen. Good luck with your writing. I can't wait to see your name on the bestseller's list."

"Thank you, Mr. Martell."

I wink at her. "Austin."

Her smile widens, and with a quick wave, I stroll into the dining room. Tonight, I'm dressed New York casual in jeans, a white shirt, a vest, and a striped tie. Wearing a tie on Whidbey Island is about as natural as wearing wingtips on the beach, but hey, what the hell. I never fit in with the locals anyway.

I glance across the sea of vaguely familiar faces and spot Stephen. He's surrounded by women, and I get it, he's a doctor, which makes him the most eligible bachelor on the island.

I've been known to bask in the attentive glow from the fairer sex now and then, but as I look across the room, I can see that Stephen's not reveling in the attention. Although he's smiling, his body language is sending a clear signal that he'd rather be anywhere else.

I know how he feels. I'm about to go rescue him when I hear a voice behind me.

"Well goddamn, if it isn't Austin Martell."

The ugly face shoved close to mine I do remember. His friends called him "the Hammer." He was the goon of the high school wrestling team. Clearly they didn't burn any gray matter coming up with that nickname, which was good because, as near as I can recall, none of them had brain cells to spare. I remember Mark Hammer stealing my lunch money. Mark Hammer shoving my head into a locker room toilet. Good times.

He's got the same mean smile he always did.

"If it isn't the guy most likely to be incarcerated. How the hell are you, Mark?"

I stick out my hand. I'm not surprised when he doesn't shake it. He raises his beer glass and I catch a flash of chunky gold jewelry. A ring with a sapphire the size of a robin's egg adorns one hand, and a bracelet as thick as a boat chain drapes around the other—gaudy, but not cheap.

"Slumming?" he asks, chugging some beer down his gullet.

I shrug, not taking the bait. "Leigh invited me and you?"

He sways back on his heels, puffing his chest out so far, I think he might topple over. He doesn't. Instead he raises his glass and drains the remaining lager. Suds pool like spit in the bottom of the cup.

"She invited me too, hoping for some deep pocket donors. Got a place on the point now," he says, bragging.

"You've done well for yourself then."

"You might say that. "

"I think I just did."

"Still got that smart mouth," he says, glowering.

A muscle in his jaw flexes and a giddy bubble of delight rushes through me. I know I shouldn't feel too pleased with myself; verbally jousting with a lack-wit is the intellectual equivalent of kicking a puppy.

"So look, you're a big shot author. You've got money, right?"

The question takes me by surprise. My mind jumps ahead, trying to figure out what angle he's working. My inclination is to blow him off, but I don't because, hell, I could use a good laugh.

"Why?"

"I've got what you might call an investment opportunity."

Does he have a brain tumor? There's no way I would invest a penny in any venture that was backed by a guy who tried to flush my head down a toilet. He's about to say more when his eyes shift away from me.

Blake Parsons's massive hand clamps down on Hammer's shoulder. A flicker of pain ripples across his face as Blake tightens his grip. Blake is not looking his usual composed self. A slight sheen of sweat dampens his brow above his bloodshot eyes.

"Austin, Leigh has you seated at a table up front." He inclines his head toward the makeshift stage. "You might want to head that way. We're going to get started soon."

By the way Blake eyes Hammer, it's clear we have at least one thing in common—neither of us has any use for this bully. Blake has given me the opportunity to break away from the unpleasant conversation, and I make the most of it.

Stephen looks up as I approach. Relief dawns in his eyes as he extricates himself from a conversation with a hopeful-looking brunette.

"I see Leigh sank her hooks into you too," I say.

"Could hardly say no. It's for the hospital."

"Where are you sitting?"

Stephen rolls his eyes and tips his head toward the table full of women.

"Think anyone would mind if I crashed your table?"

"Oh, no, no, no." An attractive dark-haired woman squeezes her way in between us. "You're at my table, handsome."

She winds her tanned arm through mine. I'll give her this—she's not shy.

"And you are?"

"Daphne Hammer."

My smile falters at the mention of her last name and she laughs.

"I know, right? I really should switch back to my maiden name. In case you're wondering, we're divorced."

I shoot Stephen a desperate look, hoping he'll intervene, but he does nothing of the sort. He claps me on the back with a grin.

"I'll leave him in your capable hands, Daphne."

She squeezes my bicep tighter than a blood pressure cuff. She steers us across the room toward a table near the stage, and I'm relieved when she lets go.

"You're here, beside me."

Daphne's waiting, like she's expecting me to hold her chair for her, and I do. I'm not dumb.

"Being an author must be so exciting," she says.

"It has its perks."

"Like being interviewed on *The Today Show*?"

"Like not having to wear pants when I go to work."

"Oh, you. You're so funny."

She slaps my arm and I wince as I reach for the bottle of wine. I pour myself a large glass. Daphne picks up her glass and I fill it too. Her eyes are psycho blue, and she's staring at me as if I am the most fascinating person she has ever met. She lays her hand on my arm and leans in close.

"I was thinking about writing a book."

"About what?"

"A single mom reentering the dating pool. It's a thinly veiled auto-biography," she titters. Inwardly, I groan.

"Have you read Nick Hornby's *About a Boy*?"

"Oh, I loved that movie. Hugh Grant was just adorable. You remind me of him," she says.

"Surely not. I have a chin."

"Oh, you." She smacks my arm again as a latecomer slides into the chair beside me. I glance over and am surprised to see Carley. She swipes a place card reading Stuart McCleary from the tablecloth and stuffs it into her purse.

"Carley," I say, doing my best to sound casual. "I didn't know you were coming."

"Usually Daddy comes to this, but he wasn't feeling well."

"Lucky me."

"So where did you disappear to the other night?"

Daphne's listening, along with everyone else at our table. Not wanting to be the topic of more island gossip, I deflect.

"I'm staying at my mom's house. It's—"

"I know where it is," she snaps.

Of course she does. She's an islander, and one of Scott's friends. The tension between us ratchets up a notch. I shoot a wistful glance toward the bar, but dammit, the Hammer is standing sentry with a drink in each hand.

"If you'll excuse me, I need to see a man about a horse."

I rise from the table and beat a hasty retreat toward the lobby. I push through the door to the men's room and take care of business. I'm washing my hands when the door to a stall opens behind me. Blake emerges. He sniffs and rubs at his nose. His startled gaze meets mine in the mirror.

"Allergies," he mutters.

His glassy eyes tell a different tale.

"Yeah, I know a lot of people in Manhattan night clubs who suffer from the same thing."

"It's not what you think."

"Yeah," I say.

"You're just like your brother. You think you're better than everyone else but..."

"You don't know what you're talking about," I snap. "Scott was..."

His mouth twists in a contemptuous snarl. "You have no idea what your brother was."

His fists curl. A vein bulges in his forehead, and he looks like he wants to hit me, but he turns and leaves before I can say another word.

I arrive back in the ballroom just as Leigh takes the stage. As poised as a gameshow host, she welcomes everyone to the annual hospital gala. Carley nudges her chair closer to mine. I do my best to shake off Blake's cryptic remarks as the salads arrive.

"I love New York. It's been so long since I've been there. You must love it," Carley says. "The theater, the culture—"

"The shopping," Daphne interrupts.

"Yes, it has all of those things," I say.

"What's it like living there?" Carley asks. "Do you ever miss Whidbey?"

The rapid-fire questions keep coming and I do my best to answer between bites of food. I'll say this—whatever is causing the resort to lose money, it's not the chef. Once the salad plates are cleared away, the salmon is served. Perfectly cooked, it is paired with a dill sauce that is so delicious, I'm plowing the last of my roasted potatoes through it as Carley fills up my wine glass. Thank god the wine is plentiful. With Daphne and Carley both vying for my attention, my head is pounding, and we're almost out of pinot noir. As if reading my thoughts, Daphne signals for another bottle.

Dessert is a silky chocolate mousse. I'm devouring it as the hospital administrator talks about the programs the proceeds from the benefit will fund.

Afterwards, Leigh announces the name of the silent auction winners. Beneath the table, Carley's leg brushes against mine. From the pointed look she gives me, I know this is no accident. I ignore the contact and angle my gaze toward Leigh, who is wrapping up her speech.

"And last up for the night, we have the bachelor auction."

Bachelor auction? Wait. What?

I shift my chair back, intending to go, but Daphne clamps onto my arm.

"You're not leaving," she says. "This is the best part."

I groan and lean back into the chair. I suppose it won't be all that bad. Compared to the poor suckers they talked into doing this, I'm getting off light.

"Tonight's first bachelor is Peter Coulter."

Peter stands and waves to the crowd. He's tall, wiry thin, with broad shoulders and a mop of curly brown hair. He mounts the stairs with the loose-limbed grace of an athlete that reminds me of my brother.

"Is your lawn full of crabgrass? Are your flowerbeds out of control?" he asks with a likable grin. "Bid on me and I'll transform your backyard nightmare into an oasis."

Leigh starts the bidding at eighty bucks and goes up at five-dollar increments.

"Do I hear eighty-five? A few hours with him and your garden will never look the same."

An older woman holds up her ping pong paddle. Three or four other women jump in, and the bid quickly escalates to one hundred dollars. Peter looks pleased as the old biddies in the crowd vie for his services.

I sip my wine. The buzz of bidding fades away as random thoughts of overgrown hydrangeas and hip-deep swaying fields of grass float through my mind. Then it hits me.

A gardener. *He's a goddamned gardener.*

I seize my ping pong paddle and launch it high into the air. An old biddy shoots me a spiteful glare.

"Three hundred dollars," I blurt.

The crowd falls silent. Heads turn in my direction. The Hammer smirks.

"I didn't know you swung that way, Martell," he calls.

A few people chuckle, and I just grin at my sudden burst of good luck. Outsourcing the yard work is a masterstroke of genius. Having this guy tame my mother's overgrown yard might just be the best money I ever spent.

"Three hundred dollars," Leigh says, cracking her gavel against the podium. "Sold to Whidbey Island's own Austin Martell."

More applause.

"Next up, Mark Hammer."

Mark springs up from his chair like he's launching off the deck of an aircraft carrier and strides down the center aisle with all the grace of a mob hit man. The polite smattering of applause dies out before he makes it on stage.

"If you need insurance, Mark Hammer's your guy. Whether it's eating dinner poolside or cruising the strait in his Catamaran, one of you lucky women is in for a fun-filled evening with this Whidbey Island bachelor."

Carley snorts. Swirling wine around in her glass, she takes a swallow. My lips quirk up into an amused grin.

"I take it you're not a fan?" I say, angling toward her.

"He's a fucktard."

A quick bark of laughter escapes my lips and I wipe my fingers across my mouth. Daphne Hammer, Mark's ex-wife, casts Carley a sidelong stare full of venom.

"Come on, Carley, admit it. You slept with him after our break up."

Carley's mouth drops wide, and she gapes across the table at Daphne, horrified by the presumption.

"Are you insane? I sold him a house, that's all."

"Me? Insane?" Daphne says. "That's rich. Don't bother lying, Carley, we all know the truth."

I'm expecting more, but Daphne makes a face and swings back toward the stage while Carley simmers beside me. The Hammer's lips peel back in a junkyard dog grin and he launches into his speech.

"Roses are red, violets are blue, I'll have an evening of romance for you," Mark says, and I groan. "First, we'll start by grilling on the deck, then a sunset cruise on Puget Sound. With wine and song, we'll finish the evening in my hot tub."

An awkward hush falls over the dining room.

Daphne raises her glass and bellows, "Take it from me, ladies, he's a real catch. Let the bidding begin."

Laughter ripples across the room. Mark's face flares red. Leigh pales. He glares at Daphne, his eyes filled with hate. Doing her best to keep things moving, Leigh clears her throat.

"Okay, ladies, let's start the bidding at two hundred dollars," she says.

Crickets.

"I bid twenty-five bucks," Daphne says. "I need my gutters cleaned."

Laughter swells around me like the rushing tide. Mark's mouth puckers like he just swallowed a lemon.

"Wait," I hear a voice call out. "He does gutters? Thirty-five."

"Thirty-five dollars. Do I hear forty?"

A hand rises in the back.

"I need my toilet snaked," another woman calls.

After five seconds of agonizing silence, Leigh closes the bidding at forty dollars. The winning bidder fist-bumps Daphne and the whole crowd laughs while Mark stomps down the stairs like a bulldozer plowing his way toward the bar in the back.

"Okay, next up, Dr. Stephen Alder. The good doctor is known for his culinary prowess, and this evening's lucky winner will enjoy a home cooked meal with the good doctor at his house overlooking Double Bluff Beach."

Standing on the stage beside Leigh with his hands in his pockets, Stephen gives the audience a humble smile.

The bidding starts out at two hundred dollars and shoots off like a rocket on the Fourth of July. Three hundred, four hundred, and the bidding's still going strong. The top two bidders glare at each other with the type of venom worthy of the Real Housewives of Coupeville.

I glance over my shoulder and see Mark Hammer knocking back whiskey from a plastic cup. I feel an unexpected twinge of sympathy for the guy. Sure, he's an asshole, but nobody likes to be humiliated.

Leigh closes the bidding at five hundred to thunderous applause. A shapely strawberry blonde wearing a floral print dress raises her hands in victory and waves to the crowd.

Leigh clears her throat and rubs the side of her baby bump, like she's fatigued. It's been a long evening. You wouldn't be able to tell it, though, from the look on her face. Blake is probably almost as anxious for the night to end as I am. He'd sooner see Leigh resting

"I've saved the best for last, ladies."

A cheer rises from the crowd and I suck back more pinot noir, wondering which poor sucker is next.

"Straight from *The New York Times* bestseller's list, give it up for Austin Martell."

10

Red wine almost shoots from my nose and I try not to choke as I swallow it.

I'm going to kill her.

It's the first thing that pops into my head when the blood finally rushes from my face back into my brain. I wave my hand and dip my head in a dismissive gesture. Everyone is staring at me, including Leigh. Carley starts to chant.

"Austin. Austin. Austin."

The crowd joins in.

"Come on, Austin," Leigh calls. "It's for a good cause."

She's put me on the spot and so, with Carley tugging on one arm and Daphne on the other, I rise from my chair. Applause crests like thunderous waves on Puget Sound as I make my way to the stage.

I stand beside Leigh and she loops an arm around my waist.

"Thanks for being such a good sport," she whispers.

Now that I'm up here, I decide to make the best of an awkward situation. I pause and gather my thoughts. A speech. It has to be a good speech. Then I have it—my hook.

"William Shakespeare once wrote, 'If music be the food of love, play on.' So on that note, we'll start our evening off at the Seattle

Symphony. Once you've been soothed by the sweet balm of music, we'll enjoy dinner by candlelight at one of the best restaurants the Emerald City has to offer. But the evening won't end there. What better way to welcome a new day than with a champagne toast at the top of the Space Needle? It will be a night to remember."

Okay, it's not my best work, but Leigh seems pleased as she starts off the bidding at three hundred dollars.

"Four hundred," bids a middle-aged blonde woman in a billowing cream dress. She holds up a paddle and eyes me with the hungry look of a fishmonger's wife.

As I look out across the assembled masses, I decide that if I'm going to be tossed around like a salmon at Pike Place Market, I might as well put on a bit of a show. So, I bend at the waist, sweeping into a deep bow, and pretend to tip an imaginary fedora in her direction.

It's then that I spot her. *Ellie.* The sight of her pretty face sends a jolt rippling through me, and I wonder why I didn't notice her before. Her gaze locks with mine. She's looking elegant in an up-do and a buttercup yellow dress. The grin spread across her face leaves no doubt that she's enjoying every minute of the spectacle.

I shoot her a pleading look, as if willing her to place a bid, but just then I hear Carley shout, "Five hundred!"

She brandishes the paddle high overhead, and Leigh claps her hands.

"Six," Daphne snaps, waving a paddle the same shade of bright red as her ex-husband's face.

I spin, turning my back on the crowd, and glance over my shoulder, doing my best to look all James Bond. The women in the crowd love it. Whistles and catcalls fill the dining room and Leigh laughs.

"Seven," Carley shouts above the din.

"Seven hundred dollars, ladies. Do I hear eight?"

I glance at Ellie and raise my eyebrows, wishing she would jump into the fray. Carley is like every other woman I know, but I'm curious about Ellie. I'd love to spend an evening with her figuring out what makes her tick. My contemplation is cut short as Daphne leaps from her seat. The paddle drops onto the table with a thwack as she raises both hands over her head.

"One thousand big ones," she screams, turning her glare back on Carley as if daring her to go on. Carley's eyes narrow and she folds her arms across her chest.

"One thousand going once. Twice. Three times. Dinner with Austin Martell sold to Daphne Hammer for one thousand dollars."

A burst of applause fills the room and Leigh pulls me close.

"You're the best. Thank you."

"You owe me."

I wink at Leigh, then quickly steal a glance at Ellie. She's embroiled in a conversation with the dark-haired man beside her, and I descend the stairs where Daphne is waiting to claim her prize.

"Mine, at last," she crows.

"My lady, your wish is my command."

I bow at the waist and hold out my hand in a courtly gesture. She places her fingers in mine and I kiss the back of her hand.

I'm about to straighten up when a fist shoots out of nowhere and slams into my temple so hard, it knocks me sideways. A constellation of stars explodes inside my head and I crash against the wall. Before I can breathe, he's on me again.

The Hammer strikes, and my knees turn to water.

"Your brother can't save you this time, bitch," he grunts.

His broad, sweating face is swollen with rage. He plows toward me like a bulldozer, heaving Daphne out of the way.

She screams and lands sprawling on the floor.

It takes three guys to restrain the Hammer. Even then, he manages to land a blow that splits my lip before I can get my hands up. Blake pins his arms back behind his head in a full nelson.

Blood fills my mouth and I fight the urge to spit it out. I swallow instead because I don't want to wreck Leigh's carpet.

"You fucking bitch. You spend my hard-earned money on him?" the Hammer screams, his words slurred.

Several women rush forward to help Daphne off the floor.

Planting her spiked heels wide, Daphne balls her hands on her slender hips.

"Your money?" she shrieks. "I earned every dime in the divorce settlement. Believe me, I earned a whole hell of a lot more than the lousy grand I spent on him."

She hooks a thumb toward me and Mark lunges for her. Blake yanks him back. A hand touches my shoulder and Leigh hands me a plastic baggie filled with ice. I press it to my face and hiss. My eye is swelling already. It hurts like a sonofabitch.

"That's enough, Hammer!"

Ellie's voice cuts through the crowd and she shoves him back. He utters a curse so vile, the middle school nuns would have popped a Tide detergent pod into his mouth and duct taped it shut.

"Why don't you ask Blake—?"

Before he can finish, Blake yanks his arm so hard, he makes the Hammer yelp. The shock of what he says hums in my ears as Ellie calls to Blake.

"Get him out of here before I call the uniforms to escort him to the drunk tank where he can sleep it off. Make sure he's not driving."

The Hammer's malignant gaze fixes on me for a second before Blake drags him out.

"Thanks," I say to an irritated Ellie, who is rapidly typing into her phone.

"You should head home too, Mr. Martell. You've caused enough trouble for one night."

Me? Trouble?

"It wasn't his fault, Chief Sharpe," Carley says. "Mark was being a drunk asshole when..."

Like a traffic cop, Ellie holds up her hand. Her upraised palm stops Carley cold.

"If I want a statement from you, I'll ask for it. Do you want to press assault charges?"

The question is directed toward me, and I shake my head.

"Nah. I've had enough fun for one night."

11

I hear pounding. At first, I'm convinced it's inside my own head, as if the Hammer is using the top of my skull for a bongo drum. I rise toward the surface of consciousness, wishing the noise would go away. But it doesn't.

It escalates, and I wake to the slow realization that it's coming from outside. I crack my eyes open a slit and my swollen eye socket throbs. With a groan, I roll over and look at the digital clock on the cable box beneath the television. 7:10, it reads. Too damned early for a social call.

I squeeze my eyes shut, doing my level best to ignore the inconsiderate sonofabitch who has chosen this moment to invade my private hell. But whoever it is refuses to go away, and the banging continues.

I throw off the afghan and rise from the couch. The cat abandons its guard post with a hellish screech and jets from the room. I trudge toward the door.

Whap. Whap. Whap. Each blow echoes inside my skull, and I grit my teeth, fully pissed.

"I'm coming," I bellow, raking my fingers through my disheveled hair as I yank open the door.

I come face to face with the last person I expect to see. Or more accurately, face to chest. Chief Sharpe is standing on my front step. She looks different in uniform.

"Uh, good morning, Chief," I say, propping my forearm against the door.

"Did I wake you?"

I grin. "Not at all. I was doing Zumba." My voice, still raspy from sleep, is a couple octaves lower than usual and I sound like Barry White.

"How's the eye?" Her fingertips graze her eye socket, as if I need to be reminded where the Hammer's blow fell last night.

"I'll live. Did you need a statement or is this a wellness check?"

"Neither, actually. I came to ask you for a favor."

"What kind of favor?"

"I want you to look at something for me."

"Now?"

I wait for her to crack a smile, but she doesn't.

"I'm not exactly dressed for it," I say and cast a gaze down at the rumpled Gap T-shirt I'm wearing and my boxer shorts.

"I can wait while you dress."

Pushy. Usually, I like that in a woman, but when the woman is a cop... I breathe out a sigh and ease away from the doorframe.

"Give me five."

"Mind if I wait inside?"

I shrug. "It's your funeral. Don't blame me if my mother's cat attacks you. I swear the beast is straight off the pages of a Stephen King novel. It's as if the Pet Sematary runs a rescue service for reincarnated cats."

She follows me inside. I leave her in the living room and head down the hall. I rummage through my suitcase and wonder what one wears to a police station. Recycling my jeans from last night, I grab a T-shirt from my suitcase and slide it on.

It's wrinkled and smells a little peaty, but what the hell, no one will care what I'm wearing. My wardrobe is a problem for another day. I forage through my Louis Vuitton for some semi-fresh socks and my running shoes. Ellie leads the way outside.

I catch my reflection in the police cruiser's window. My shiner is almost completely hidden by the lenses of my shades. I climb into the passenger's seat beside Ellie and she pulls out of the driveway.

"So, what's going on?"

"I know this is highly irregular, Mr. Martell, but I was hoping you'd be willing to consult on a police matter."

Consult? Me? Why?

"This isn't about the thing with Hammer last night, is it?"

She doesn't look my way, but the slight twitch of a muscle in her jaw tells me that I've struck a nerve.

"Hey, look. I was only kidding about the Hammer. He was drunk. I think he was pissed at all the attention his ex-wife was lavishing on me."

"So, what did you do last night after the auction?"

"I came home."

"By yourself?" she asks, one eyebrow cocked as if she has good reason to ask.

I wonder if it was Rob or Carley who's been spreading gossip about where I sleep and with whom. I flip my hands over in a careless, palms-up gesture.

"Yeah. Why?"

"Can anyone corroborate that?"

"You mean other than my mother's psychotic cat? You see, Chief, the problem with heading home alone is that you're *alone*."

She ignores the sarcastic witticism and focuses on the road. The miles disappear in a blur of blacktop and evergreen trees. Bypassing downtown Coupeville, we head west toward Penn Cove. I gaze out toward the stony coast. Low-hanging clouds touch the gray sea, and the wind spikes the water into waves.

My gut snaps as tight as a rubber band as I see flashing red and blue lights fill the driveway of the gaudy McMansion perched on top of a hill. Every cop on Whidbey Island must be there.

"What's going on?"

Ellie doesn't answer. A grim-faced cop stands sentry at the bottom of the driveway. Recognizing the chief, he waves us through. She parks her cruiser at the end of a long line of first response vehicles.

"Stay here," she says.

I watch as she confers with a detective. I assume he's a detective because he's not in uniform. His sharp gaze cuts past her to where I'm sitting. He gestures toward where I'm sitting, and I can see that he's not happy she brought me here, and frankly, neither am I.

Though I can't hear what she's saying, I see him nod. He still looks pissed, though, as she heads back toward the car.

"Whose house is this?" I ask when she opens the passenger's door and steps back to let me exit the vehicle.

"You don't know?"

"How the fuck should I know? I haven't lived here for fifteen years. In the two days since I stepped foot on this godforsaken island, the only places I have been are the hospital, the Willows, and my mother's house."

"And the police station. You forgot to mention that," she adds.

She's making a point and I know it. We all omit little things. But this...

"Put these on." She hands me a set of police-issue latex gloves.

I should argue, but I don't. I pull the gloves on and trail after her, past the cop guarding the entrance to the backyard. As we push through the squeaky gate, my stride begins to slow.

"Chief Sharpe."

She ignores my summons and gestures for me to keep up. We skirt the edge of the huge lawn, and all at once, I see it.

My stomach heaves, and I know why the cops are here—why I'm here.

A white sheet is spread out across a lumpy mass on the concrete patio. It's not just a mass. It's a body. And I know whose body it must be.

Mark Hammer's.

Cold fingers of fear squeeze tight around my throat, and I stare at the puddle of crimson blood pooled on the patio in horror. A wave of nausea broadsides me, and instinctively, I sprint across the lawn. Away from the body. Toward the bushes.

Cops are yelling at me as I skid to a stop by a thick stand of rhododendron bushes and heave. Gone is last night's salmon in its delicious dill sauce. Gone is the wine. Bile burns the back of my throat and I prop my palms on my thighs as I pant through my mouth and wait for the nausea to subside.

The dank smell of the earth and vomit fills my nostrils. I heave again, but nothing comes up. After a few moments, I wipe my mouth.

"You okay?" Ellie asks.

"Yeah."

It's a lie. I'm not okay. I'm sickened, and shaking, and I want to go home.

"I thought all you mystery writers were used to seeing crime scenes."

I straighten away from the bushes, my spine as rigid as steel. "For your information, Chief Sharpe, I write fiction. Cozy mysteries. Not thrillers, or police procedurals. My stories are the kind of books with a nice, neat body. No blood. No gore."

"I want you to look and tell me what you see."

"You mean besides the dead body."

She nods. Reluctantly, I pull in a deep breath. The cold morning air fills my lungs and I force myself to look.

"Okay, so you already know who the victim is."

"Mark Hammer. Yes. What else?"

"Well, obviously, he fell from that balcony."

I point toward the balcony above the patio. French doors branch off from what I assume to be the master bedroom.

"You think he fell, or was he pushed?"

"Pushed?"

A chill that has nothing to do with the cool air blowing off Puget Sound races up my spine. We must be breaking all kinds of department policies here. But she doesn't seem to care.

"You saw what kind of shape he was in at the auction. What's to say he didn't come home, hit the whiskey hard, and stumble over the edge?"

It's plausible, I tell myself, though the writer in me whispers that there is more to this story.

"Hammer's a heavy drinker. I don't see a couple shots of whiskey sending him over the edge."

"You can't possibly think that I did this."

The expression on her face gives nothing away.

"I asked you to consult. Is there anything else about the scene that strikes you as odd?"

I huff out a breath and refocus, aware that Ellie is watching me.

There's a bottle of wine and two glasses sitting on the table. I take a closer look. The wine is from a local vineyard. Cheap. One step up from Two Buck Chuck. Not the kind of thing a pretentious ass-hat like the Hammer would serve. My stomach drops as the realization hits me. Cheap wine. Red roses in a vase. I can tell by the heavy fragrance, they're Mister Lincoln roses.

I pick the bottle up in my gloved hands. Shake it. I hear the sluggish rattle of something heavy shifting inside. The bottom of the bottle is filled with coins. I set it down with a thud, my heart racing.

It's just like I wrote it.

"It's like a scene from one of my books."

"*For Love or Money,*" she says. "What do you make of that, Mr. Martell?"

I swallow. "I don't know."

"You don't know?"

"Look, I thought Mark Hammer was a narcissistic douchebag, a bully, but I didn't kill him. Based on his legendary charm, I have no doubt that half the island hated his guts. Besides, what possible motive would I have for wanting him dead?"

"He hit you."

"Please. If I tried to publish a book where the motive for murder was a quasi-high-school brawl, I'd be laughed out of New York. Would you kill someone because they hit you and then be stupid enough to stage the murder in a way that would bring the police to your door?"

"We're not talking about me."

She shoots me a pointed look, but I don't rise to the bait. I'm not afraid of awkward silences. Reconciling herself to the fact that I'm not going to blurt out a confession anytime soon, the chief continues.

"I guess the real question is who would want to kill Mark Hammer and implicate you?"

"I suppose that's your job to figure out, Chief Sharpe. I haven't the faintest clue."

12

Officer O'Brien, a husky cop with a blond brush cut, is assigned the dubious honor of driving me home. I spend half the ride trying to decide if I should call a lawyer. And though I'm certain there were dozens of people who won't be crying at Mark Hammer's funeral, Chief Sharpe landed on my door this morning.

I should at least call Diana and let her know what's going on. She'd know what to do. As soon as the thought enters my mind, I dismiss it. After throwing a hissy fit, she'd have me whisked off to a non-extradition treaty with an internet connection so I can work on the next book.

If I hadn't gone to the auction, I wouldn't have seen Hammer, and if I hadn't seen him, I wouldn't be in this mess. Desperate for something to take my mind off the horrible crime scene, I strike up a conversation with the cop. I'm always curious about people.

"How long have you been on the force?"

"Seven years. Joined up after I left the military."

"Did you enlist after high school?"

He nods. "My dad was retired Air Force."

"What do you think of her? Chief Sharpe?"

He lifts his hand off the wheel in a half-shrug. "She's good. A pro. Some people think she got the job because of her dad but..."

"Her dad?"

"He was chief of police back in the day."

I find it interesting that both she and O'Brien followed in their fathers' footsteps.

"What's she like?" I ask.

O'Brien looks at me as if I'm the dumbest person who ever lived. "I don't know. She's the chief."

We run out of conversation long before he drops me off at my mother's house.

I enter through the kitchen door. It's been a hell of a morning, and I need to do something to take my mind off the bloody crime scene, so I start sorting through the mountain of mail heaped on the kitchen table. I pitch the junk mail into an empty box and stack the legitimate-looking stuff in a neat pile.

Despite my best efforts, my mind drifts back to Hammer. The fact that the crime scene was staged rules out suicide. So, who would hate him enough to send him over the railing and plunging to his death?

As a mystery writer, I know that motive is the key to unraveling any crime. Why would someone want to kill him? Money? From the look of his house, he wasn't hurting for cash, and he made a big deal of the fact that he was considered a "deep pocket donor." But knowing Hammer, that could have been bullshit. All bullies put on a good show. What if he had gambling debts? What if he was into something illegal? What if he was so busy making himself look important that he was swimming in debt?

If money was the motive, the police will know. They will be all over his finances.

So, what else is there? Love? The thought of Mark embroiled in a love triangle makes me laugh loud enough to startle the cat.

Not love. Sex?

If it was sex, he was paying for it, and if that was the case, he was probably hooking up in Seattle. There are no secrets in a small town.

Before long, the box is brimming with junk mail. I'm about to pick it up when the cat comes screaming into the room. And by screaming, I mean that he's mewling. Loudly.

"What?" I snap.

He clearly wants something. And then it dawns on me. Food. I may be a little slow, but I'm not stupid.

"All right. Hold on," I mutter and march to the cupboard.

There is more cat food than human food in here. I shake my head. My mother must still equate starvation with good health. How many lectures did I get about overeating? She'd pinch my muffin top and shake her head in disgust.

I am not buying you new clothes because you're too fat to fit into your jeans.

A spark of anger ignites inside my chest, and something else— shame. The way she'd looked at me, as if I were a lesser life form because I didn't look the way she thought I should, like Scott. It's not like I didn't get harassed enough at school.

The cat mewls again.

"Yeah. Patience."

I rip the lid off the Fancy Feast tin and place it on the floor. The way the cat dives in fills me with remorse. He must be starving. I should set a reminder on my phone to feed him. Living alone, I sometimes forget to eat, but the way the cat's hip bones jut out from beneath his scruffy coat is not healthy. It's sad.

Speaking of phones, I jump when mine goes off. If it's Diana calling to nag me again, I swear I will lose my shit. But it's not Diana. It's the hospital. With a sinking feeling, I pick up the call.

"Austin, this is Stephen."

"What's wrong?"

"It's your mother—she's awake."

I THOUGHT I was ready for this, but I'm not. By the time I enter the hospital, I'm vibrating with nerves. I barely hear Mrs. Newman's greeting as I race down the hall.

The nurse finishes taking her vitals and leaves the room. My mother turns her head slowly as I step inside. Our gazes meet. A look of shock floods her eyes.

"Scott," she croaks.

I flinch. The sting of her words drives me back a step and I struggle for something to say.

"It's your other son."

"Austin?"

She looks confused. Scared. I know the right thing to do is to take her hand, but I can't bring myself to touch her. Like two magnets pointing north, the history between us repels us apart.

"The hospital called me when you had your...accident."

"Accident...?"

"You took a blow to the head. You've been unconscious for a few days."

She looks around the hospital room, as if trying to reconcile her recollections with her surroundings, before her gaze finally settles on me.

"You've...changed," she says, still sounding a little out of it. "I... didn't expect..."

Expect what? That I'd come? That I'd look so much like my dead brother? There are a thousand ways she could finish the sentence, but she doesn't. Neither of us do. We're both so careful about what we say it's like we're stepping between landmines, trying to find the safe places, keenly aware that any misstep could destroy what is left of our relationship.

"Do you remember what happened the night you...fell?" I ask.

A troubled expression crosses my mother's face.

"No."

Her voice trails off. I force myself to do the thing I've been resisting ever since I walked into this room. I take her hand. Her warm, waxy fingers are rigid in mine. I was a kid the last time I held my mother's hand—a terse tugging across the street. The contact feels uncomfortable. Foreign. I give her fingers a quick squeeze before releasing them and jam my fists into the pockets of my jeans.

"It's okay," I say. "You hit your head pretty hard. Temporary memory loss is not unusual."

She pales as the words sink in. I'm making a mess of this. I'm scaring her. Not comforting her. Scott would have known what to say.

"Seriously, Mom. It's nothing to worry about." I shift my weight from one foot to the other as an oppressive silence builds. "How do you feel?"

"Awful."

I nod. "No doubt. Get some rest. I'll see you later."

She sinks back into the pillows as I leave her bedside, heading for the door.

"Austin," she calls.

In one of my stories, this would be the turning point—the heartfelt moment between two characters that acts as a catalyst to bridge a burgeoning emotional gap and heal a broken relationship. I turn back toward the bed, half anticipating, half dreading what she will say next.

"Austin," she whispers.

"Yes?"

"Did you feed the cat?"

13

I need groceries. It's one of those stupid, fundamentally human things you need to do to survive. Eat. Sleep. And shop. The parking lot is less than half full and I pull my car into a spot not far from the entrance.

I forgot how gorgeous the produce was here. There are so many farms on the island that the markets are filled with fresh vegetables, apples, and pears. I pick up a ruby red tomato and gave it a sniff. It still smells like it was just plucked from the vine. I grab a few of them on my way toward the lettuce.

A pair of middle-aged women dressed in puffy vests and yoga pants stand by the apple bin, their heads tipped together. The way they whisper so intently reminds me of high school girls discussing boys, or other girls, or the basketball game, or whatever the hell it is that high school girls talk about.

The topic of conversation they've fallen upon looks decidedly unpleasant. I see the residue of it on their faces—in the scrunched eyebrows, pursed lips, and frown lines. They look up and catch me watching. Their eyes widen, as if a known felon has entered their midst. All conversation stops.

As if they are members of a synchronized swimming team,

they turn their backs in choreographed harmony. I instinctively know they're talking about Mark Hammer. Do they know I'm a suspect?

I move from the produce aisle over to dairy and pick up some fresh milk and eggs. Placing them in my basket, I head over to the meat section. Bacon is a rare treat I allow myself when I've finished a draft or done something good. I hear my mother's voice as clearly as if she was standing beside me.

Do you know how much fat there is in bacon?

Guilt is hardwired into my brain. Bacon is bad. Bread is the enemy. These thoughts would never occur to me in New York, but now that I'm here, the sight of food triggers them at every turn. My mother would never order bacon. So I do the only logical thing I can do—I order myself a full pound.

The guy behind the counter wads the fatty meat on top of the waxy paper, and with a slight shiver of shame, I drop it into my cart. I soothe my conscious by choosing whole wheat bread and head for the cash register posthaste. The clerk rings up my purchases and I leave the store, bags in hand. The doors slide closed behind me when I see it.

There's a white paper pinned beneath my windshield wiper. It flaps in the breeze. My city instincts kick in, and I become hyper-aware of my surroundings, scouring the parking lot and the alleyway for a stranger lurking in the shadows, but near as I can tell, there is not another living soul in sight. Of course, mine is the only car that's been tagged.

I don't like this. I'm typically not paranoid, but it's as if the parked cars have eyes and they're watching me. Sounds crazy, I know. But after seeing the Hammer's body under a tarp...

Stowing the groceries in the back, I yank the pinned paper free. It's not a flyer, like I first thought. It's a page torn out of a paperback book.

Oh, shit. It's from my book.

This is not good news. Not only has some homicidal maniac staged Mark Hammer's murder to look like a scene I wrote, now someone is leaving notes on my car. I scan the page. It's a love scene from *For Love or Money*.

Whoever has left it on my car has drawn a thick red heart around a witty exchange between two characters destined to end up together at the resolution of the story. I suppose I should be relieved that they didn't leave a murder scene, but still... Someone followed me here and left this note for me to find.

At the very least, it's creepy.

When I call the police station to speak to Chief Sharpe, she's not there. I figure that she, along with half of the force, are still out processing the murder scene at Mark Hammer's house. Since this technically isn't an emergency, I leave her a message.

On the way back to my mother's house, I spy a roadside coffee shop and pull in. The smell of fresh coffee and croissants makes my mouth water. Damn, I'm hungry. The pastries displayed behind the glass look so good that it takes all my willpower to resist. I'll make an egg white omelet at home, I tell myself. Protein instead of carbs. Sticking fast to my resolution, I order a cappuccino.

I'm standing by the counter waiting for my drink when I spot a familiar face. Dark hair frames her pale cheeks, and she's wearing the biggest pair of Chanel sunglasses I've ever seen. She spots me, waves me over, and how can I resist? After all, if I'm the police's number one suspect in the slaying of her ex, she's got to be number two.

Daphne Hammer does not remove her sunglasses as I straddle the chair opposite hers. Her cup clatters noisily against the saucer and she cringes as people look our way.

"How are you holding up?" I ask.

"You've heard?"

"Everybody's heard." At least, I assume they have, the small-town gossip network being what it is.

"You're not afraid to be seen with me?"

"Why would I be?"

"The police think I did it."

"It's standard procedure for the police to check out the ex," I say to ease her concerns.

"We've been divorced for years, and yeah, I hated the bastard, but I would never kill him."

I hear the tremor of stress running through her voice and I reach over to pat her hand.

"Love and hate are two sides of the same coin. Besides, we can't be the only two suspects on the island. Your ex wasn't exactly a loveable guy."

"We? You too?"

"What do you think the chances are that there is anyone on the island who hasn't heard about our fight?"

When she laughs, I laugh too, because you know what they say— misery loves company.

"Dammit, why am I letting them get to me? I've done nothing wrong. We will not let them intimidate us," she says, finally removing her sunglasses and setting them on the table.

"Preach it, sister."

"So, when are you picking me up?"

"Huh?"

Okay, she's lost me. I'm all in for the rah-rah-girl-power part of the speech, but now the topic has shifted meaning in a way that leaves me flat-footed.

"What time are you picking me up? You know, for our date?"

Date?

The sudden turn of conversation takes me by surprise, and for a moment I'm rendered speechless. Trust me, that doesn't happen very often. And then it hits me. *The bachelor auction.*

"Don't you think the timing is bad? I mean..." I shrug like it should be obvious. I'm not even sure that by now her ex has made it to the morgue.

"You're not going to welch on me, are you?"

Welch?

"I'll pay you back."

I would gladly pay a thousand bucks to steer clear of this mess, but the way Daphne's jaw sets, I know that she's in no mood to relent.

"I don't want money. I bought you fair and square."

She's got me pinned and she knows it. I let out a sigh and incline my head in a reluctant nod, knowing full well that this is a bad freaking idea.

"Good. Well then. What time are you picking me up?"

"Tonight? Maybe we should wait a few weeks."

Daphne eyes me with a narrow look.

"How long are you staying?"

She's got me there. Now that Mom's awake, putting together a plan for her care just got easier. And I've got a book tour to get back to. The sooner I can get back to New York, the better.

"How about six?" I ask.

"How about four? We'll need to catch the ferry to America."

"America?"

"Well, duh," she says, rolling her eyes. "I didn't pay a grand for you to take me out to Flyers."

She's right. We can't stay on the island. The only thing worse than taking a dead man's wife out on a date is being *seen* taking her out on said date.

"See you at four," I say.

Suddenly, I have quite a lot to do.

14

"You all right? You seem kind of tense," Daphne says as she settles onto the vinyl bench beside me.

She must have spent hours on her hair and makeup, and it's paid off. She looks gorgeous in a black halter dress that leaves her brown shoulders bare. My hands clench into fists as the ferry lurches away from the dock and we're underway.

I feel the vortex of panic start to form, and this time, Ellie's not here to save me. While Daphne may be willing to perform a little mouth-to-mouth resuscitation should the need arise, I'd rather not put that theory to the test. I need a distraction.

"I was thinking about your ex," I say.

"Don't. I spent most of the morning with the police trying to figure out who hated him enough to kill him. I mean, who didn't want to kill him? It's not like he was a handsome charmer like you."

Her response tells me that she's not going to want me to rehash what she told the police. I choose my tack carefully, picking the most likely motive.

"Did he win the Powerball or something? I mean, that house..."

"Oh, that. Yeah. He knows a couple of mortgage brokers. He

picked it up on a short sale when the housing market tanked. From her."

"Her?"

"Carley Darling."

Well, shit. That wasn't what I was expecting her to say. It sounds like a plausible explanation. So much for my drug dealing theory or some kind of get rich scheme.

"But that Catamaran he bought must have cost a fortune," Daphne says. "I don't know how on earth he swung that."

"He had a Catamaran?"

"Yeah. Those things can cost upwards to a million, though I'd guess his was somewhere in the low six-figure range."

"That's a lot of money. Where do you suppose he got it?"

She shrugged. "It could be leveraged to the hilt. Money ran through that man's hands like water. Sailing's his passion, so..."

The casual mention of the boat reminds me of Rob and Cameron's diving trip.

"Did Mark dive?"

Daphne nods. "He was an expert. He taught me."

I want to ask more, but our conversation is cut short by the blast of the ferry horn. It's time to head back to the car. At least this time I made the crossing without having a meltdown, and I've learned a curious new fact about Mark Hammer.

"I need coffee before we dock. How about you?" Daphne asks.

I don't need anything that might make me more jumpy. I decline, and Daphne heads off toward the café while I pull out my phone. I dial the number of my forensic accountant friend. Thank God he answers quickly. This is one conversation I don't want Daphne to overhear.

"Hey, Craig, I was wondering if you could do me another favor."

"Sure. Shoot."

"I don't have time to explain right now, but I need you to look into something else for me."

~

THANK GOD WE LEFT EARLY, because Seattle traffic is a full-blown horror show—wall to wall cars from the time we hit the highway all the way into downtown. Skyscrapers block out the golden rays of the sun. Daphne flips for valet parking. The relief I feel at being out of the traffic turns to pleasure as we step into the beauty of Benaroya Hall. The cylindrical design of the lobby provides stunning views of Puget Sound, the Seattle Art Museum, and the city skyline.

For a second, it's like being back in New York. There isn't a stitch of flannel or a pair of Crocs as far as the eye can see. Feeling more at home than I have since I landed on the island, I smile down at Daphne.

"Would you like something to drink?"

"Champagne."

She cozies up against me. I feel her warm body press against my arm. I know full well what she's up to, and I don't mind playing along. A little flirtation never killed anyone.

"Consider it done."

After all, what kind of date would I be if I didn't fetch some champagne? She did pay a ton of money for my services; I should at least make it worth her while.

Daphne heads to the restroom as I thread my way through the clusters of people on my way toward the standup bar.

A couple hundred voices blend together in a harmonious blur of sound. Then I hear it—bright and clear, like the high tones of a flute cutting through the din. She laughs, and I turn.

It's Chief Sharpe. Only tonight, she doesn't look like Chief Sharpe. Tonight, she is definitely Ellie.

She looks as elegant as Audrey Hepburn in a lovely blue lace dress. It skims across her shoulders and curves enticingly between her breasts. I know I'm staring, but I can't help it.

Ellie turns her head toward me. Her eyes lock onto mine. My heart jolts, and for a second, it's like we're the only two people in the room. A hint of a smile plays at the corners of her lips.

What is she doing here? Did she follow me? And when she sees me with Daphne Hammer, what's she going to think? That the two of us were conspiring to off her ex?

"Sir? Sir?"

An elbow jabs into my ribs. I realize the line has moved on and it's my turn to order.

"Two glasses of champagne," I say to the bartender, and he snaps to with a sharp nod.

Daphne's not back from the restroom yet. I shoot a glance over my shoulder and see Ellie walking toward me.

"We've got to stop meeting like this," I say.

She flips her hair off her shoulders and meets my ironic gaze. "What brings you here, Mr. Martell?"

"Mr. Martell? So formal. What happened to Austin?"

"You're here with Daphne Hammer?"

She doesn't miss a thing.

"The symphony seems like an odd place for a stakeout, don't you think, Chief Sharpe?"

She arches an eyebrow above her lovely brown eyes, but she doesn't answer.

I sigh. "I'm fulfilling my bachelor auction duties. You know what they say, a Lannister always pays his debts."

I bow stiffly from the waist. Ellie's shrewd grin tells me that she's a *Game of Thrones* fan.

"Ah, yes, the bachelor auction that started the brawl."

"I'd hardly call that a brawl. Don't you have a murder to solve?"

"My team is on it. They know where to find me if the need arises. By the way, did you leave me a message earlier today?"

I'm so distracted by the fullness of her lips that her question takes me by surprise.

"What? Oh, yeah. I found a note on my car today."

"Where?"

"Under the windshield wiper."

"I mean, where were you parked?"

"At the grocery store," I reply with a sheepish grin.

"What did it say?"

"There you are," a man says.

He approaches Ellie with two drinks in his hands. Is he her boyfriend? I wish he was a ghoul with bad facial hair and acne scars, but he's not. An inch or two shorter than me, he has a lean build, short hair, and a narrow face. Neither handsome, nor hideous, he's decidedly average.

He hands Ellie a champagne flute, which she accepts with a smile.

"Greg, this is Austin Martell."

He offers his hand, but my hands are full. I raise the champagne flutes with a what-are-you-gonna-do kind of shrug.

"Good to meet you," I say.

It's a total lie. Champagne won't begin to take the edge off the confounding buzz of irritation I feel at seeing the two of them together. I sip from my glass and pretend not to notice as his free hand moves to the small of Ellie's back.

"How do you two know each other?" Greg asks and takes a sip of his drink.

"I'm a suspect in her murder case."

Poor Greg looks so shocked, he almost spits out his beer. He shoots Ellie a curious glance.

"Tell me, Greg, how do you know the lovely Chief Sharpe?"

"We met through a few cycling club friends," Ellie answers for him. "Greg's got season tickets to the symphony. So, tell me about the note."

I don't want to tell her in front of Greg. I'm only slightly relieved when I see Daphne approach.

"You're the last person I expected to see here, Chief Sharpe," Daphne says.

"Not half as surprised as I am to see the two of you...together."

Daphne's expression sours. I hand her a champagne flute and she takes a sip. A strained silence falls between the group. There isn't time for much more when the gong sounds, signaling that in a few minutes the performance will begin.

"They're playing our song," I say to Daphne. "Greg, it was good meeting you."

"You too." He flashes a half-hearted grin.

My gaze lingers on Ellie before Daphne tugs me away.

"You don't think she's following us, do you?"

"Unfortunately, I think she's on a date."

I didn't mean to say the *unfortunately* part, but Daphne doesn't seem to notice. She shoots down the champagne like it's tequila and I try not to cringe.

"I suppose that makes sense. It's not like she can date on the island. There's nothing sexy about a woman who carries a gun for a living."

Ellie's smart enough to intimidate most men. And her job... Being a single woman and a chief of police would be tough anywhere, but on a place like Whidbey, it would be doubly so. We're on our way back toward our seats when the flash of a camera temporarily blinds me. A slim blonde introduces herself.

"Austin Martell, right?"

"Right," I say, still seeing spots.

"Annabelle Taylor, entertainment reporter for *The Seattle Times*. What brings you to town, Austin? A book tour?"

"Visiting family," I say.

"Welcome to the city. If you've got time for an interview..."

She folds a business card into my hand. I thank her and keep going. I should call her and ask if she will Photoshop out the black eye. Best not to mention it, otherwise the story will be less about me and more about the black eye. And the dead guy who gave it to me.

We make it back to our seats just in time for the lights to dim. Daphne settles in close beside me and the orchestra starts playing the opening notes. But my mind is still on Ellie, and the way she looks in that dress, and I know that Daphne's wrong.

There is something sexy about a woman who carries a gun.

15

It's four in the morning New York time when I drop Daphne off at her house. Extricating myself from her with a simple good-night kiss on the cheek is more difficult than it sounds. I skillfully dodged her invitation inside for a night cap and head back to my mother's house.

Immediately upon entering the kitchen, I sense that something isn't right. I flick on the kitchen light. Someone's been in here. Either that, or there's been a landslide on Mount Rainer. Half the contents of the junk mail tossed haphazardly on the table have been dumped on the floor.

I hear a noise toward the back of the house. The hairs on the back of my neck prickle

The cat. It's got to be. The last time I freaked out about an intruder, it was the cat making all that noise. I blow out the breath I've been holding and berate myself for being such a wimp. I'm going to name the damned thing Cato, after Inspector Clouseau's manservant, trained to attack at random intervals as a way of keeping the inspector's fighting skills sharp.

"All right, show yourself," I demand.

Cats never come when called, and true to form, this one is no different. It continues to lurk in the back of the house as I make my way down the hall, knowing full well where it's hiding. My mother's room.

I stride down the hallway when I notice something strange. The door to Scott's room is open a crack. I reach for the handle. The door opens halfway before it crashes back into me with tremendous force. I block it with my forearm, but the blow knocks me off balance. My head cracks against the frame. A bolt of pain shoots through my skull.

My eyes are blurry with tears as someone lunges toward me. Black pants. Black shirt. Black mask. Big. A boot sails toward my head. Connects with my cranium. Bright sparks of pain burst behind my eyelids. And that's it. Darkness engulfs me.

I don't know how much time has elapsed before I come to. Luminous green eyes stare down at me. I yelp. Shift. Throw the thing off. Cato lets out an ear-splitting yowl. White hot pain splits through my head and I gasp.

I press my palm to the side of my head. It comes away sticky with blood.

"Jesus," I mutter as I struggle to push myself off the floor.

The room spins for a second or two. I wait until the spinning stops before sliding across the hallway to brace my back against the wall. The pounding in my head expands as I call 911.

I'm cramming ice cubes into a Ziploc bag when the cops arrive. Officer O'Brien, the cop who drove me home, is on the doorstep. I don't recognize the two other cops. O'Brien takes the lead.

"Walk us through everything."

I sigh and press the ice to my temple, trying to focus my thoughts.

"There was an intruder. Big."

"Like my size?"

I shrug. "I guess. It was dark. I didn't get a good look at him."

"Where was he?"

"In my brother's room."

The police enter Scott's room while I trail behind. I catch sight of myself in the mirror. Between the black eye and the cut on my head, I look like the victim in a bad horror movie. I'm going to make quite an impression on my book tour—that's if I make it back to New York.

"Anything missing?"

"Who can tell?"

It's as if a tornado has ripped through the place. Dresser drawers hang open. The contents of the closet have been tossed. Trophies have been toppled. Broken. Photographs torn.

O'Brien's radio squawks and he steps out of the room. Without the cops here, I am alone in Scott's room. It's the first time I've stepped foot inside it since I got back. Standing here among his things tears a hole inside me.

Growing up, I wanted to be Scott. He was handsome, smart, the consummate athlete. The trophies once displayed on the top shelf of his bookcase are strewn across the floor. Instinctively, I head toward them.

I probably shouldn't touch anything before the cops have completed their investigation, but I can't help myself. Being in here is like connecting with a piece of my brother again.

The largest of the trophies is broken in half. I set the ice pack down on the bookcase and pick up the two pieces. I fit the halves together as if such a simple act could make them whole. I remember when he got this. It was his last year of high school and he had led his team to their third championship title. Most Valuable Player. 2003. Scott Martell.

And he was. Most valuable. My room became the dumping ground for unwanted things, but Scott's room is a shrine. It's as if time stopped the day he died. The contents of his room were never packed away. Hell, there's even a stack of folded clothes sitting on the chair beside his desk, coated with a layer of dust—as if Mom couldn't bring herself to come in here either. Sixteen years later, she's still waiting for him to come home.

I startle at the sight of Ellie in the hall.

Gone is the dress she wore only hours ago. Instead Ellie enters the room wearing dark jeans and a long-sleeved T-shirt. Her hair is pulled back in a ponytail and I see the bulge of a gun at her hip.

"Are you okay, Austin?"

"I guess."

"You guess?"

"You should see the other guy," I joke.

Ellie doesn't crack a smile. She's eyeing the gash in my head with a look of concern I find endearing.

"What happened?"

"He was in here when I arrived home. I heard a noise. Thought it was the cat."

"Why don't I have one of the guys drive you to the hospital?"

"I'm fine."

"Is that your expert medical opinion?"

"I'm not a doctor, but I play one on TV."

She takes the pieces of the trophy out of my hand and places them on the bookcase. She picks up the ice bag and hands it to me, her gaze locked on mine. Staring deeply into my eyes, she frowns with a slight shake of her head.

"You could have a concussion."

"How can you tell?"

"You're even less funny than usual."

It hurts to smile. Ellie sighs and scans the room. I can tell by her expression that she gets it—the way my mother has been holding onto the past, to the memory of her dead son with both hands, unable to let go.

"You should see my room," I joke.

She cocks an eyebrow. "Really?"

"Oh yeah, she's erected a shrine. Books. Newspaper reviews. Magazine articles. It's embarrassing really."

"Chief," O'Brien calls from the hallway.

Ellie nods toward the door. "We should let them do their thing."

I follow her out into the hall. My heart skips a beat when I see the door to my room wide open. She glances inside. And stops, as if transfixed by the dumpster fire of my room. A stab of shame pierces me deep. I press the icepack to my throbbing head and move past her through the kitchen toward the living room.

I see Cato peer around the edge of the couch as I sit. Closing my eyes, I lean my head against the wall and empty my mind of everything besides the throbbing pain. It's easier to focus on the physical pain then the rush of feelings that threatens to surface at the thought that my own mother cares more about her dead son than the one who is still alive.

It's a small house. The deep voices of the cops travel through the thin walls as they sort through the mess, looking for clues. God knows what they're going to find in there.

I drift, lose track of time. Thinking about my brother and me. Memories that I've kept locked inside for almost half my life, unable to do so for one minute more. It isn't until I hear the softer sound of footsteps approach that I snap back into the moment.

Ellie lowers herself into the chair beside the couch. We're close. Our knees are inches apart.

"The guys are finished for now. We're going to send a tech over in the morning to dust for prints."

"Think you'll find anything?"

"I hope so. How are you holding up?"

Ellie shoots me a pointed look I can't ignore, and I know she's asking about more than my physical well-being. Her eyes are a warm golden brown, filled with compassion. I look away and set the baggie filled with half-melted ice down.

I've never told anybody what my mother said to me the day of Scott's funeral. It's too painful. Too humiliating. I've always been astounded by a parent's unique ability to wound those they're supposed to care about the most.

As if sensing my thoughts, Ellie lays her hand on my arm.

"Sometimes grief brings out the worst in families. Your brother's death was a huge shock to both you and your mother. I know how it feels. My father died of a heart attack when I was in college. He was a big, strapping guy. A cop. Never sick a day in his life and then..."

She trails off with a shrug.

"It took me years before I could talk about it, until the pain of the loss receded to the point where I could breathe again. Some families pull together in tragedy while others break apart."

I absorb this in silence. The warmth of her fingers curled around my arm is a comfort. I don't pull away.

"Your mother lost a son, Austin, but you lost a brother. I can only imagine how hard that must have been for you."

Her words level me. No one has ever said that to me before. A bolt of sorrow stabs me so deep I can't utter a word. My eyes film over with unshed tears. The silence that falls between us feels profound. A shared pain.

Officer O'Brien appears at the door and Ellie pulls her hand away. It drops to her side.

"We're heading back to the station, Chief."

"Right."

She follows him from the room and I head down the hall. I stop by the bathroom to splash cold water on my face and rinse the blood from my hair. The cut stings like a bastard. When I finally emerge, the other officers have gone. Ellie's in the kitchen, scratching Cato. He's purring. I open a fresh tin of cat food and place it on the floor.

"Do you have any idea what the thief was looking for?"

"In Scott's room? Not a clue. I suppose I could ask Mom. She's awake."

Ellie nods. "I know."

Of course she knows. She's the chief of police.

"I hope I didn't interrupt your evening," I say.

"What?"

"Greg."

"Oh, no. He lives in Seattle."

"That's good," I say.

I hadn't figured him for an islander. I'm more aware of her than I should be—the way the subtle scent of her perfume lingers on her warm skin like a caress.

She turns in the doorway with a questioning look. I hold her gaze. There's an unexpected tenderness to the moment—a result of what we shared. I wonder if she feels it too. I'm struck by the most insane impulse to kiss her right now, but I don't dare. I don't know how she will react. And after all, she is carrying a gun.

"My team will sort through the evidence they collected tonight. I'll be in touch."

She opens the door. Pauses.

"I really do think you should go to the hospital, Austin."

"I'll be fine."

"I can send a patrol car by if you're worried that the intruder might return."

"Or you could just stay here," I say. "For protection, I mean."

I'm kidding, of course. Well, sort of. Ellie doesn't rattle easily, but gauging from the shocked expression that crosses her face, I've managed to knock her off her stride. She opens her mouth to respond, but I cut her off with a grin.

"Not to worry, Chief Sharpe. I've got my trusty attack cat to guard me. We'll be fine."

16

I hear pounding. And it's not my headache. Someone is at the door. I should be used to these early wakeup calls by now, but hell, it jars me awake.

I glance out a window half hoping to see a police cruiser parked out front and Ellie at my door. Instead, I see a white Karmann Ghia. It takes a second for me to place it. *Carley.* I haven't seen her since the night of the bachelor auction. She's looking ridiculously perky in the bright morning light.

"Oh shit. I woke you," she says.

"I may forgive you if that's for me."

Carley lifts the cup of coffee toward the screen door and I can almost smell it. "It *is* yours. How do you take it?"

"Black."

"Whew. That's easy."

She stands on the step with an expectant look on her face.

"I'd invite you in, but the place looks bad and smells worse."

"You should see some of the places I have to deal with."

"You say that now, but I swear..." I make a face and she giggles. "What brings you by?"

"It's a gorgeous day. I was wondering if you'd be up for a drive."

"A drive? Now?"

"It's only fair to warn you—I'm a morning person. That's why I brought coffee."

I weigh the options between coffee and sleep. Then I open the front door. Carley bubbles with enthusiasm as she hands me the cup. The sundress she's wearing looks like it's made for her. The airy white fabric sets off her summer tan and strikes the right balance between tasteful and sexy. I'll admit I'm staring a little when I catch her wrinkling her nose in disgust.

I shouldn't have let her inside. Before I know it, the town will be buzzing with stories about how Mom lives.

"Sorry about the mess. Apparently Mom's been having some health issues."

I clear a stack of magazines off a nearby chair so Carley has a place to sit. She hesitates a moment, as if she's afraid to mess up her pretty white dress, before taking a seat. I peel off the plastic lid of the coffee cup and take a swallow. It smells good and tastes better—deep and earthy. I could bathe in the stuff.

My gaze drifts across the piles of junk scattered around my mother's living room.

"I'm working at clearing the place out before Mom gets home from the hospital."

"It might be easier to burn the place down."

There is nothing ironic about the callous remark. The abruptness of it startles me, and I laugh.

"Sorry. Sometimes I'm a little too honest. If it were my listing, I would fully expect to sell it to a buyer who would level the structure and build something new."

I get it. She's a realtor. She sees everything with an eye for profit, not the life my mother has lived here—her desperate attempt to cling to the memories of Scott.

"I doubt my mother would see it that way."

The silence between us grows uncomfortable and I change the subject.

"How about something to drink?"

I can't recall if I bought anything to drink other than the milk I picked up at the grocery store yesterday. Probably not.

"Not necessary," Carley chirps. "I had a banana ginger smoothie after my workout."

"You worked out already?"

"Yeah. I'm learning how to kickbox."

"You? Kickboxing?"

"You don't think women can be tough?"

"I didn't say that. I'm just surprised."

"I've been doing it for six months now. It's great cardio. Blake is teaching me."

"Blake, as in Leigh's husband?"

With a slight shake of her head, Carley laughs. "Seriously, Austin. How hard did Mark punch you?"

I grin. "Not that hard. Does Blake teach a class?"

"No, but he's a qualified personal trainer, a real slave driver, actually. But thanks to him, I can actually do ten pull ups now."

"There's a special place in hell reserved for editors, and personal trainers," I quip.

I want to ask her if Leigh knows about the private lessons but think better of it. There's no point in stirring up trouble. I'm sure Carley knows that Leigh hates her guts.

"So, about that drive?"

"Where to?"

"I could tell you, but then it wouldn't be a surprise."

She shoots me a playful look and I grin. Rob doesn't know what he's talking about. Carley may not be the brightest woman I've ever met, but she's harmless. And it's not like I'm looking for a relationship. I won't be here that long.

"Why not? Let me grab a quick shower."

I leave Carley in the living room and head toward the bathroom. True to my word, it only takes me five minutes to shower and brush my teeth. I knot a towel around my waist and curse myself for not remembering to bring some clothes with me. My suitcase is in the living room.

While Scott and I were not the same size when we were in high school, we're probably close now. Ignoring the slight pang I feel as I enter his room, I drop my towel. A jolt of shock courses through me at the sight of Carley inside. She looks just as shocked at the sight of me, naked as the day I was born. I snatch the towel off the floor and cover up.

"Sorry," she says. "Occupational hazard. I was curious about the rest of the house."

"It's okay, but I have to warn you, my mother's ninja cat likes to hide under the bed."

"I've handled worse things than a cat."

Her gaze drops to the hastily knotted towel around my waist with a grin. The tension between us builds and I know what she's thinking. And while part of me is tempted to repeat the booty call we answered the other night, I woke this morning thinking about Ellie, and it's the thought of her that stops me from giving Carley what she wants.

She picks up on my hesitation.

"I'll wait for you outside."

I rummage through Scott's drawers to find something to wear. I find a pair of cargo shorts and a T-shirt. They fit well enough. I pull on socks and my loafers as I head out the door.

The sun has broken through the layer of fog. It's going to be a fabulous day. Carley smiles when she catches sight of me.

"What?"

"Is that Scott's shirt?" she asks.

I look down. The high school crest is emblazoned on the chest and I shrug. Carley starts the car and we head inland.

"So, where are you taking me?"

"You're really not good at surprises, are you?"

All right, if she doesn't want to tell me, I'm not going to pry. I relax back in the seat and let the warm wind wash over me.

A flurry of evergreens flashes by in a blur. In my desperation to escape the claustrophobia of small-town life, I've forgotten the beauty of this place. Now, I see it again through fresh eyes. I want to explore the deep, green recesses of the forest, drink in the pastoral beauty of the farms, watch the sun sink into the Pacific until the sky turns black.

It's not like me to be this sentimental. I couldn't get out of here fast enough, but now, this place is starting to grow on me. It's a disturbing thought.

The car turns west, and the shallow, silver waters of the Admiralty Inlet shimmer in the morning sun. An enormous shingle-styled Victorian poised alone on the edge of the beach looks as if it were transported straight from the East Hamptons. The crisp white trim pops against the weathered cedar shingles. And though some people would easily see this as their dream home, the writer side of my brain tugs me in the other direction.

Tacked to the corner of the deck is a discreet "For Sale" sign. A twinge of apprehension shivers down my spine as Carley heads straight for it.

"What are we doing here?"

"You've got to see this place. Come on. You're going to love it."

I'm not the kind of guy who claims to have a psychic connection, but there is something off about this place. I feel it the second I follow her though the door, inside the massive kitchen. I take in the high ceilings and hardwood floors.

"It has ten bedrooms. And that's not counting the two in the service wing."

"Service wing?"

"You can't run a place like this yourself," she says, heading down the hallway.

Our footsteps echo down the hallway. I pause inside the doorway leading to the great room.

"This one room is bigger than my whole condo."

"Then you need more space."

More space?

"You obviously don't know the size of my royalty checks, but they're nowhere near this roomy."

Carley smiles. "Well, you might be surprised. First, you're on Whidbey Island, not Long Island."

"Yeah, but..."

"This place has been on the market for years. It's a killer deal."

"Next you're going to tell me about the young family that was killed here and how nobody wants to buy the place because it's haunted."

Carley looks at me as if I've lost my mind. "They say that writers have good imaginations, but honestly, Austin... Of course it's not haunted. It's owned by a tech millionaire from Seattle. As far as I know, he's still very much alive."

"Look, even if I was planning to stay, which I'm not, what would I do—what would anybody do with this much space?"

She sweeps her hand toward the French doors that open onto a huge patio. Panoramic views of the Sound can be seen from every side.

"You could host parties. Invite your New York friends."

Chuckling, I shake my head. There is no way my New York friends would fly all the way here. To do what? Hang out with the locals? Meet my mom? The idea is so ludicrous, I don't even know where to begin.

Carley leads the way up the curved staircase off the main entrance. Reluctantly, I follow. She stops to show me each of the bedrooms until we reach the master.

The white French doors overlook Useless Bay. Opening them, she steps out onto a small balcony and motions for me to join her. I don't want to go out there, but I do. From the corner of my eye, I catch a flash of color. Red. A riot of late summer flowers is in bloom on the patio below. I catch the heavy scent of roses carried on the breeze.

And just like that, the scene at Mark Hammer's house comes rushing back. I remember the balcony with the wrought iron railing, the bottle of red wine on the table, a lumpy form under a white sheet, trails of blood on the patio stones. The roses.

"We should get going. I have some writing to do."

"I haven't shown you the best part yet."

There's more?

A cold gust of wind bursts off the Sound and I shiver. Carley locks the French doors and crosses the bedroom toward the hall. I gaze longingly toward the staircase, wanting out of this house, but Carley heads in the other direction.

There's a circular stairway at the end of the hallway that leads to the third floor.

"What's up there?"

"See for yourself."

The sooner we do this, the sooner we can leave. The staircase leads up to a turret room. The windows face southwest, offering a sweeping view of Useless Bay.

"Isn't this amazing?"

"Sure."

Carley ignores my indifference as she drifts toward the center of the room with a dreamy look on her face.

"Don't you think this would be the most amazing nursery? Can't you just picture it, Austin? A crib here. Change table there."

A nursery? Kids? What?

While I'm standing here thinking REDRUM, she's busy laying out the nursery. This is no idle daydream. Intuitively, I know that she's been here before. She's probably spent hours in this room constructing a whole fantasy life, complete with a husband and a baby. The only babies that would be birthed here would be gruesome little Chucky dolls.

For the first time since I landed on this godforsaken island, I'm relieved when my cell phone rings.

Jaws.

I could kiss Diana right now.

Carley turns toward me with a questioning look.

"It's my agent," I explain. "I have to take this. I'll meet you outside."

17

"Austin! Where in the hell have you been?"

"I'm sorry, Diana. With everything going on here..."

Infusing each word with a gravity worthy of James Earl Jones, I let the sentence hang.

"How is your mom?"

"She's not out of the woods yet."

I suppose I should feel guilty about making things seem worse than they are, but I need some reason for my lack of productivity. And seriously, it's not like this has been a vacation. It's been mentally exhausting being back. With the shape my mother's house is in, it's amazing I don't have bronchitis from the dust and mold in there. I'm not entirely sure that bronchitis is trigged by environmental factors but...

"You must be very worried," Diana says.

"Yeah," I agree and blow out a sigh.

"Well, it's good to see you're not spending all of your time cooped up in the hospital."

Wait. What? I'm struck by the immediate sense that I've just stepped into a carefully constructed trap.

"What do you mean?"

"Imagine my surprise when I see a photograph of you in *The Seattle Times*. How was the symphony, Austin?"

Oh, crap. I didn't think they'd run the photo. To be honest, I didn't even check.

"Well, you see, that's a story—"

"Where are my pages?"

I'm momentarily stunned into silence.

"I'm holding off the Mystery Network, but they won't wait forever, Austin."

"I understand."

"Do you? I hope so, because this is a once in a lifetime opportunity."

"I know. Thanks, Diana," I say, doing my best to sound contrite.

"And another thing, Austin, stop ignoring my texts. You know it drives me crazy when you ignore my texts."

"Yes, ma'am."

"Your first book signing is in five days. When will you be back?"

"Give me a few more days to sort things out."

The silence on the other end of the phone is deafening. I can feel Diana's frustration building, and I get it. She's worried that I won't make it back in time. But now that Mom's awake, figuring out what kind of care she needs is about to get easier.

"If you're not going to make it, I need to know. Don't leave me hanging, Austin."

I promise I won't and I'm relieved when she says goodbye. I slide the phone into my pocket as Carley locks up the house.

"How's your agent?" she asks.

"Demanding."

"That's why she gets paid the big bucks."

"I suppose so."

We climb into the car and back up the windy road. I avoid watching the house grow smaller in the rearview mirror. As much as I try to deny it, the conversation with Rob is still niggling at the back of my mind. I wasn't going to ask, but in the silence, I can't stop myself.

"I heard something the other day."

Carley's face brightens. "Oh, what kind of something? We real estate agents hear all the best gossip—who's having an affair, who's breaking up. So, spill."

"You said that your husband left you."

A shadow ripples across her face and her expression hardens. "And?"

"And I know this is crazy, but someone said he was missing."

"Missing? Let me guess. Leigh."

Her voice is filled with venom, and I could bite my stupid tongue off. It wasn't Leigh, but telling her that would only make her dig until I revealed Rob as my source. And then I'd have to explain that I called him when I left her house in the middle of the night. I'm not willing to go there.

"I'm sorry. I did warn you that writers are curious souls. You don't have to tell me what happened if you don't want to."

"And let Leigh spread her lies?"

From the way Carley's fingers drum the steering wheel, I can tell she's agitated, and I wish I'd had the damned fool sense to keep my big mouth shut.

"Missing? I suppose he is. That bastard ran off without a word— no goodbye, no forwarding address, no money. He wanted out and didn't have the balls to tell me in person, so he ran away."

"I'm sorry, Carley. I shouldn't have said anything. It's none of my business."

Carley's foot stomps down on the accelerator and the car's engine roars. Gravel spits out from beneath the tires. I clench the armrest tight.

"Leigh thinks she's perfect. She thinks she knows everything about everyone, including her precious Scott—"

The unexpected utterance of my brother's name jolts me.

"Scott?"

Carley yanks the wheel and we make a dizzying hairpin turn onto my mother's road. She accelerates up the hill like we're being chased. I want to tell her to slow down, but she's already angry and I don't want to piss her off more.

"I'm sorry. I didn't mean to upset you."

"It's not you. It's *her*," Carley says. "She couldn't accept the fact that Scott loved me."

"What?"

"Scott. Yes. The last summer he was home..." Carley's face contorts with equal measures of anger and pain. "Leigh refused to let him go. She has everything, and I have nothing. It's not fair."

Carley slams on the brakes. The car skids to a halt outside my mother's house. I reach for the seatbelt buckle and scramble out of the car, careful not to slam the door. She doesn't say goodbye as she pulls out of the driveway and takes off down the road.

Shell-shocked, I watch her go.

18

The house is as quiet as a tomb, and in the stillness, the ghosts of the past are restless. Scott's death is like a wound that won't heal. I'm not the only one who feels the pain of his loss keenly. The animosity between Carley and Leigh is as raw now as it was a decade and a half ago. What did she mean about Leigh not letting Scott go? The brother I knew was devoted to her. He never would have cheated on Leigh. Would he?

I drift down the hallway toward Scott's room.

It still looks like a tornado tore through here. I see the pieces of his MVP trophy on the bookshelf.

The pieces of Scott's life are scattered at my feet. I bend. Sort through the rubble. There's a snapshot of Scott in his football uniform. Leigh is tucked into the crook of his arm, beaming up at him with a look of pure adoration.

I've probably seen this photo dozens of times, but never once did I notice Blake in the background, his hair damp with sweat. And while Scott looks like he's never been sacked, Blake looks as if he's been dragged across the field. His uniform is stained with grass and mud. Carley, dressed in her cheerleading uniform, is pressed against his side, but he's not looking at her. It isn't that that makes my blood run cold. It's the way he's looking at Leigh.

I jump at the buzz of my phone ringing. My heart plummets as soon as I see the hospital's number come up on my call display.

"Austin, it's your mother."

Everything after those words blur together in a surge of panic.

I remember the word "setback," and not much else. It's as if the shock has distorted my senses in a way that makes it difficult for me to grasp the meaning of the words. I tuck the photograph in my pocket as I leave the house.

Big fat drops of rain smack into my windshield. My pulse redlines as the car fishtails, and my hands clench the wheel in a death grip, fighting for control. I steer into the skid until the car rights itself. The hospital lies dead ahead.

I pull into the first empty stall I see and slam the gearshift into park.

You're not even in a legal parking spot, my mother's voice caws inside my mind, but I don't care.

There is no one manning the volunteer desk as I race down the hall toward my mother's room. I screech to the door and freeze as I peer inside. She's not there. Her bed is empty and I...

Conflicting emotions crash into me. Dread. Relief. Guilt. There is no time to process the onslaught of all I feel when I hear a voice behind me.

"Austin."

Stephen is standing there looking pale and grim.

I struggle to push the single word out past the lump of emotion clogging my throat.

"Mom?"

"She's in intensive care. She's had a stroke. I've administered a plasminogen activator."

"What?"

"It's a drug that works to dissolve a clot and improve blood flow to your mother's brain."

A stroke. Good Christ.

"What happens next?"

"We're doing what we can."

Stephen interprets my tortured expression as grief. He squeezes my shoulder in the way guys do when they're offering comfort.

"Want to go see her?"

He doesn't wait for my answer. We traverse the hallways in grim silence until we reach the ICU. I gaze through the glass at my mother's withered form and wonder what will happen to us. Will she live? Die? Will we ever get the chance to set our relationship to rights? Is that even possible?

I feel lost, disoriented in the swell of emotions that overwhelm me.

I barely hear Stephen introducing me to the nurse at the duty desk. She must be used to dealing with shell-shocked family members. She leads me to my mother's bedside.

"You can talk to her, you know."

"Can she hear me?"

The nurse, whose name I have already forgotten, gives me an encouraging smile. "I like to think so."

It's not really an answer, and I stand there, feeling helpless and drained. Unexpected tears well in my eyes, and I'm not ready for this. I force myself to take her hand the way Scott would have done if he had been here instead of me.

"I'm sorry this happened to you." My throat aches as I choke out the words, wondering if she can hear. "I never wanted this for you. If you can hear me, you've always been tough. Fight your way back."

Mom lies there, still. Unmoving. After a time, I release her hand and sink into the chair beside the bed. In the quiet of the room, with only the sound of the beeping monitors keeping time with the thudding of my heart, I think about my mother. And me. All the things we've said. All the things we have done that brought us here to this point—the ocean of pain that lies between us.

My head tilts back. I close my eyes and wonder, if this were a scene in one of my books, how would I want it to end? I know what my readers would expect—forgiveness. Repentance. Reconciliation.

But how do you forgive the kinds of wounds that live deep inside your heart? There are words so painful, so cutting, that they can never be taken back.

In the years since I left, I have done my damnedest to forget all the things she said.

But forgive?

I drop my head into my hands, knowing the kind of man I want to be, trying to find the goodness inside of me that would allow me to let go of the bitterness that has pooled inside my heart, filling the special place reserved for a mother's love.

Tears leak from between my tightly clenched eyelids and I wipe them away.

The soft squeak of rubber-soled shoes pulls me from my thoughts. I drop my hands to my sides. The nurse is back. She eases into the room with an apologetic smile.

"Your mother needs her rest."

"Of course."

I stand, gazing down into my mother's face, searching for the hereditary markers that connect us. I see my brother's shadow in the curve of her brow, the sharp cheekbones that jut beneath her sagging flesh, and I realize that maybe that's the closest we'll ever come to being a family. Maybe the only thing that connects me to my mother is our shared memory of Scott. Without him, we are rudderless, solitary beings searching for something that no longer exists.

The smell of sickness overwhelms me. I have to get out of here.

I hurry toward the doors and jog to the car, and just like that, I'm gone. My eyes are on the road as my inner thoughts follow their own painful paths. Families are complicated. Some are havens—safe harbors where you can always find love. Acceptance. Others are rocky shores. My family has been shaped by our losses. Isolated by them. While crisis draws some families together, it has splintered mine apart. I'm a wreck, left adrift, with no place to go, and no one to go home to.

I pull into the driveway for the Willows without fully intending to. Too many raindrops to count drill into the roof as I sit, staring blindly out the windshield, wondering if this is why I came home—to bury the last of my family.

Time gets away from me as I allow my thoughts to drift. Then someone knocks on my window. I almost jump out of my skin.

Leigh is crouched down, peering through my window. Her arms are folded, and she's wincing against the driving rain as if every drop hurts. Blonde hair is plastered against her skull.

"What are you doing out here, Austin?"

I lift my hands in a wordless shrug.

"Come inside."

I exit the car and dash up the stairs behind her. Inside the lobby, she brushes the wet hair out of her face. The look on my face stops her cold.

"What is it? Your mom?"

"She's had a stroke."

"God, Austin. I'm so sorry. Come inside."

I tell her that I need a drink and lead the way to the bar. The first martini goes down far too easily, as does the third. Leigh is pouring the fifth when I see her bristle. I turn my head to catch a glimpse of Carley hanging onto Blake's arm.

She's wearing a killer red dress with a narrow waist and a flared skirt that looks like a throwback to the fifties. Her chestnut curls have been tamed into a sleek ponytail. She reminds me of someone. I'm trying to figure out who when Leigh sucks in a quick breath.

"Why can't she leave him alone?"

"Do you mean Blake or Scott?"

She recoils in shock at the sound of my brother's name. The vodka has loosened my tongue enough that I don't care. I barrel ahead, heedless of how callous I'm being.

With an angry look, Leigh plants her hands on her hips and lets me have it. "That whore spent the summer before Scott died breaking us up."

"What happened?"

"He and Blake went to a field party, you know, the one they hold on Memorial Day out at Patterson's farm?"

I nod. It's not like I ever actually went. I just heard about it.

"So, I was away that weekend. Scott got drunk, I mean like, really drunk, and Carley...Carley was there..."

"So, Scott slept with Carley?"

She nods, tears bright in her eyes.

I'm still trying to accept this. Scott loved her. Of this, I have no doubt.

"How did you find out?"

"Blake told me."

"Blake told you?"

Okay, I may not know exactly how the best friend thing works, but I can imagine that the general rule of thumb goes something like this—if you cheat on your girlfriend and your best friend knows it, they don't tell your girlfriend about it. They lie. It may be a lie of omission, but it's a lie just the same.

"Why?"

"Why what?"

"Why did Blake tell you?"

I see the outrage fill Leigh's face.

"Why wouldn't he? It was the truth."

"What happened after Blake told you?"

"What do you think? I broke up with Scott."

"Wait. No. That didn't happen." Scott and Leigh never broke up. I'm sure of it.

"For that summer, we broke up. Carley hung off him all summer, but he kept trying to get me back. It wasn't until..."

"Until what, Leigh?"

Leigh's twists the wedding band violently around her finger as she formulates her thoughts.

"Until he proposed to me."

"You got engaged to Scott? When?"

Tears fall down Leigh's cheeks and she brushes them away. "The day the boat sank."

I know that brothers don't always share everything, but seriously, how did I not know this? What else don't I know about Scott's life prior to the accident?

"Why do you think Blake told you? About Carley, I mean?"

"Because he was my friend too."

"That was noble of him," I mumble.

I don't know whether Leigh hears me. She's mixing another martini, and I remember what Blake said to me the night of the bachelor auction. I pull the photo I found in Scott's room from my pocket. I set it on the bar. We were all so young then. None of us had the faintest clue how our lives would turn out—not Leigh, or Scott, or Blake. I stare at the photograph, transfixed by the expression on Blake's face.

Did Leigh know that Blake was in love with her? Did Scott?

19

My head feels like the pulsing speaker of a sub-woofer, expanding and contracting to the throbbing beat of a bass player on crack. And worse still, my mouth tastes like dead squirrel. I admit, I've never actually eaten a dead squirrel, at least not one with its fur still on, but it's the first image that comes to mind.

I know I should call the hospital and check on Mom, but I'm not ready to do that yet. I need coffee first. That's the only hope I have of limping my way through the blitzkrieg of pain exploding inside my head. In order to make coffee, though, I'd need to get out of bed, and right now that seems only fractionally less appealing than opening my eyes. Resigned, I roll to my left.

And fall. Okay, I've never had exceptionally quick reactions. Scott was the jock in the family. I got three black eyes playing basketball by not getting my hands up in time to stop the orange leather orb from smacking me squarely in the face—not all at once, obviously. Three black eyes in a lifetime, not including the one the Hammer gave me. I guess that makes four.

My forehead takes a nice bounce off the cork tile. Great, now I'll have a scuff-mark on my forehead to go along with my fading black eye. At least it wasn't hardwood, marble, or slate. Wait.

Cork?

It takes a second to register.

Where the hell am I?

Now I force my eyes open. Blinding morning light stabs my eyes like the blazing beam from an interrogator's floodlight and I squint. Clearly, I'm not on my mother's couch.

I open my eyes a little wider and push up onto my knees. The couch I just vacated is the most comfortable thing I have slept on all week. It's cream colored with a pattern. Peonies I think. Behind the industrial white pillowcase, I catch sight of a sage green throw pillow. A little romantic for my taste but...

Aw, Christ. Carley.

Reflexively, I look down. At least I'm still wearing boxer shorts, and I woke up on the couch. That's got to be a good sign, right? Judging from my monstrous hangover, it's quite likely I was too drunk to do anything worse than make an ass out of myself.

Bracing one hand on the couch and the other on the coffee table, I push myself up. The room spins in a death spiral, and I slap my hand against the wall. It takes a full ten dizzying seconds to regain my equilibrium.

I don't remember much about Carley's house. It was dark when I left. The place looks cleaner than I would have thought. I don't mean the lack of dust. I pictured Carley as a clutter-girl, with knickknacks and photographs everywhere.

A couple of deep cream armchairs are grouped in a cozy cluster around the coffee table. Books line the wall next to the river rock fireplace. It all looks neat and orderly. A huge mirror hangs above the mantle where a television would usually be, and the detail strikes me as odd.

I never figured Carley for much of a reader. Wincing, my bare feet slap the cold cork floors as I make my way over to the bookshelves for a closer look, because I can't help myself. I'm always curious about what people read.

I scan the list of titles to get a sense of genre. Again, I'm surprised by what I find. Legal thrillers, mysteries, and suspense. No fifty shades of trashy romances sully the shelves. I stop when I encounter my own. I pluck my first book off the shelf and find myself flipping toward the back, to the page that was torn out and left on my windshield. It's there.

The relief I feel is short lived as I hear the tick-tack of toenails approach.

The big, hairy, saber-toothed canine glaring at me must weigh over a hundred pounds. It's not just a dog; it's a goddamned German Shepherd. Its lips are pulled back in a menacing grin, and I catch a flash of freckled, pink gums above a line of fierce-looking teeth. Its tail is not wagging. A coarse fin of brown and black fur juts between its shoulder blades. I'm no dog whisperer, but it doesn't take a genius to know that none of these signs bode well for me.

I raise my hands. "It's okay, nice doggie, you don't have to kill me," I say, when the dog's owner comes into view.

Another shock ripples through me, and Ellie laughs.

"Usually I have to point my gun and yell freeze before a man gets his hands up in the air."

"Very funny," I say in a voice that sounds more like Kermit the Frog's than my own. "Call him off."

I know the tremor in my voice is not very manly. What little control I have over my bodily functions is spent preventing myself from pissing down my leg. Amusement lights Ellie's eyes as she lays her hand on the dog's head. The grinning stops, but I'm convinced the dog is still sizing me up for breakfast. I force my hands to my sides, but I can't take my eyes off the beast.

"You're afraid of dogs?" Ellie says, shaking her head with mock incredulity. "Isn't the hero of your books a veterinarian *with* a dog?"

"A highly intelligent beagle, not some mutant goon attack dog."

"An intelligent beagle? That's an oxymoron," she laughs again. "Relax. Daisy wouldn't hurt a fly."

The absurdity of pinning a name like Daisy on the four-legged killing machine would seem laughable if not for the vice grip of fear constricting my airway.

"He looks hungry."

"She." Ellie scratches the dog behind her ears, and her tail starts to wag. The hackle is down. I release my breath out in a huff. It's only then that I realize I'm standing nearly naked in her living room. We seem to notice this around the same time as her gaze rests on my boxer shorts.

The corners of her lips tug up.

Now what? It's cold in here.

Then I realize I'm wearing my Mickey Mouse boxer shorts. They're a little quirky, I'll admit that, but they're comfortable. Not something I would typically plan to be seen in, but I wasn't expecting a sleepover.

"Nice," she says, with a smirk.

I stumble toward the couch and stoop to pluck my jeans up off the floor. I'm trying to think of a witty comeback but come up empty.

Toenails tapping, Killer jogs through the kitchen and sits by the door and emits a high-pitched whine that sets Ellie in motion.

"We're heading out for a run. I'd ask if you want to join us, but you don't exactly look up for it."

Laughter fills Ellie's eyes and I wonder how bad I look. I rake a hand through my disheveled hair.

"There's coffee in the kitchen if you can find it. I'll give you a ride home when I get back."

She looks smaller out of uniform, the runner's tights hugging her trim thighs nicely. Her sleek, auburn ponytail swings like a pendulum as she exits through the back door.

Left on my own, I start to snoop. I'm usually pretty good at pegging a person's personality type by glimpsing their habitat. This place was a stretch for Carley but is nothing at all like I imagined Ellie's home. I was expecting a small gray apartment, sparsely decorated. Not this bright, open beach house. It's tasteful, warm. I don't know the Ellie that lives here, but I would like to.

The kitchen is small, but well laid out. In no time at all, I have coffee brewing. Craving some fresh air to blow away the cobwebs inside my aching head, I step out onto the deck to admire an unobstructed view of the Sound.

The cool air feels good on my clammy skin. The tang of the saltwater air fills my lungs. Pulsing waves of gray water scale the stony beach then recede. The steady rhythm of the waves provides a soothing counterpart to my pounding hangover, and I rest my forearms against the railing. In the distance, I see Ellie and her beast.

She runs like a woman on a mission, not someone out for a friendly jog. The sleek figure slicing through the morning fog reminds me of the Terminator—the silver one from the second movie. Her long strides are fluid. Intense. Full-on. Ellie runs the same way she approaches her job—with laser intent.

The beep of the coffee maker summons me inside. Ellie's refrigerator is well-stocked. I pull out the fixings for one of my famous omelets and place them on the countertop. Okay, they're not exactly famous, but they should be. In the back of the fridge, I spy something even better. Tomato juice. So, I go looking for its partner in crime. I know I'm half in love with Ellie when I find a bottle of vodka stashed in the freezer. A little hair of the dog should set me back to rights.

The Bloody Mary is already working wonders when Ellie bursts through the back door. Killer eyes me like I'm an intruder. She keeps her large body positioned between me and Ellie, like I can't be trusted. Ellie must notice it too. Taking no pains to hide her amused grin, she tosses the dog a couple of treats and Killer snaps them out of the air. Satisfied, she licks her lips and Ellie nudges the dog out of the way. Crossing the kitchen, she arches an eyebrow as she leans toward the stove to examine the contents of the pan. The perfect omelet is almost finished.

"You cook?"

I smile at the skepticism in her voice.

"Those of us who don't have *real* jobs need to do something productive to fill our time." I pick the pan up off the stove and slide the contents onto a plate with a flourish. After adding a generous dollop of salsa and sour cream on top, it's ready to go.

I hand the plate to Ellie. She's about to argue when I pour the next batch of beaten eggs into the medium-hot pan. With a shrug, she finds some cutlery and settles on a stool at the island. I pour her a cup of coffee and set it beside her plate.

Surreptitiously, I watch as she takes the first mouthful. Her eyes widen then roll back into her head. I smile. That is the exact look I was going for. Feeling absurdly pleased with myself, I drain the last of the Bloody Mary.

"What did you put in here?"

"Just some stuff I found in your fridge."

"God. I haven't eaten anything this good in ages."

"You need to get out more."

Her eyebrows arch, but she doesn't disagree, and soon we're hunched over the countertop eating side by side. It feels oddly natural sitting here with Ellie, and I'm enjoying the peaceful moment. I'll need to remember every second of this once I'm back at the hospital.

"So, tell me, Chief Sharpe, how did I end up here last night?" I ask in a teasing tone.

"Leigh called me."

I can't tell if she's joking. Her expression is inscrutable, and I don't remember much after the story about Scott.

"I've got to hand it to you small town cops, that's service. Do you drive all drunk out-of-towners home?"

Ellie allows herself a small smile.

"Just the famous ones. Besides, we've got a homicidal maniac running loose on the island. Imagine the hit my reputation would take if you end up on a slab down at the morgue."

"So, you've decided it wasn't suicide?"

"Yes."

I wad another forkful of omelet into my mouth as I let this sink in. Hammer was murdered. And someone broke into my mother's house. Twice. And someone is leaving me notes. I need to figure out what it is that binds all these events together. Soon. Before things escalate any further.

"Got any leads?"

Dodging the question, Ellie shrugs. "How's your mom?"

I wince and push my plate away.

"She had a stroke last night. I'm not sure how bad."

"Oh, Austin. I'm sorry."

Ellie lays her hand on mine. The heat of her palm warms my skin and I don't pull away.

"Are you okay?"

I nod. "You've probably figured out that we're not close and I'm... I know how I should feel...how I do feel...but..."

I gaze into Ellie's face, wishing that I had the words to express the complex tangle of emotion filling me, but I don't. The morning light slants in from the window, illuminating the copper highlights in her hair, and I am struck by her quiet beauty—so different than Carley's, so different than any woman I have ever known.

Her eyes are sprinkled with cinnamon and gold. A lock of hair falls into her face. I brush it away. My fingertip lingers on her skin, and I am drawn to her, overcome by the need to kiss her. Her eyes close, her lips part, and I...

Her cell phone rings. She jerks back, and the spell is broken as she picks up the offending device.

"Sharpe." The shift in tone is unmistakable and sends a shiver of alarm shooting through me. "I'll be right there."

"Bad news?" I ask when she hangs up.

Ellie doesn't answer. She stands abruptly and dumps the remainder of the omelet into the sink.

"We're out of here in five minutes. I'll drop you off at your place."

"I should head to the hospital." I stand and look around for my coat.

What coat? I didn't bring one from New York, and I haven't gone shopping yet. I pat my pockets and find my wallet. No keys or cell phone, but it's a start.

"You've got enough on your plate. I'll find my own way there."

Ellie props her hands on her narrow hips and eyes me skeptically. "I'm pretty sure you don't know where I live."

"True, it's been a decade and a half since I set foot on the island, but I think I can figure it out."

"Suit yourself," she says.

20

I start off down the beach with my hands shoved deep in my pockets. About the time my skin turns blue from the chilly wind off the water, I break into a slow, lumbering jog. The desperate attempt to jump-start my body's natural heating system doesn't last long. The combination of egg, Bloody Mary, coffee, and last night's vodka sloshes around in my gut and forces me to slow down before I donate my breakfast to the gulls.

I breathe through my mouth to settle my stomach. As I round the point, I see the Coupeville wharf in the distance and I realize I'm a few miles outside town. I'm an ass. I should have taken Ellie up on her offer. What kind of idiot leaves his cell phone in the bar? Oh wait. I know the answer to this one.

A vicious blast of wind shoots off the Sound. I rethink my plan to follow the beach. Cutting between the houses, I head down a narrow easement that joins up with the main highway into town.

The cold air clears the fog from my brain and I find myself thinking about Ellie. Why didn't she dump me off at Mom's place? It would have been the easy thing to do. Maybe she realized I didn't have my keys with me. Whatever the reasons, I'm glad she did. She probably saved me from ending up with Carley. Again.

As I trudge along the side of the highway, I dismiss the notion that she might care about me the second it enters my mind, before it has time to take root in my vodka-addled brain. Ellie sees me as superfluous, the kind of guy who lives a make-belief life. I'm not the kind of guy she could respect, let alone care about.

The problem is, she may be right.

When was the last time I put someone else's needs in front of my own?

I'm knee-deep in self-pity when a Mercedes Coupe goes whizzing past. Icy droplets spray off the damp road. Goosebumps as big as gravel speckle my arms. The brake lights flare and the car squeals to a halt. I see the driver's face reflected in the rearview mirror.

There is a god. And he drives a Mercedes.

I jog up the road and open the passenger's door. Stephen takes one look at me and cranks up the heat. Checking the mirror, he pulls back onto the highway. I rub my hands together in front of the vent.

"Where have you been?"

The terse tone of Stephen's question takes me by surprise. My stomach drops.

"Why?"

"It's your mother."

"How bad?"

He shakes his head. And just like that, the bottom drops out of my world.

"I'm sorry, Austin."

"You mean she's...?"

My throat closes. I can't bring myself to utter the words. Stephen says it for me.

"She's gone."

∼

I DON'T REMEMBER the rest of the ride to the hospital. The blood roars though my ears and I float along, suspended somewhere between shock and pain. Stephen stops the car and we sit there in silence for what seems like an eternity.

"You okay?" he asks.

"Yeah."

Like a zombie, I trudge down the hallway behind Stephen. Mrs. Newman spots me and rises from her chair. Tears shine in her eyes.

"I'm so sorry, Austin," she says.

She wraps her arms around me. I feel her fragile shoulder bones beneath her sagging flesh. After a second or two, I pat her back and pull away.

"Thank you."

"If there is anything I can do..."

I nod.

Stephen is waiting for me at the door to the ICU. The nurse is the same one who was on duty yesterday.

"She's in there," the nurse says softly. "Take your time."

I don't want to go inside. It's too much reality to face. Stephen rests his hand on my shoulder. It's the nudge I need to get my legs moving. The door closes behind me and I jump at the hollow sound.

No longer tethered to the plastic tubes and leads that connected her to the medical equipment, Mom is free at last. The morning I first arrived on the island, I was shocked by how small she seemed, and now...she seems to have shrunk even more. She looks like a stranger. A hollow dread fills me as I move to the bedside and stare down into her face. The silence presses in.

And everything hits me then. The finality of it all. She will never open her eyes. She will never speak, or laugh, or cry. The last words we ever spoke to each other were about feeding the cat.

I wasn't ready for it to end this way. I am adrift in a sea of grief with nothing to grasp onto—no final memories of reconciliation or forgiveness. An emptiness consumes me because deep inside, I'm still the boy who needed to hear the words, "I love you. I'm proud of you." No matter how old you are, those words matter, and not hearing them—never hearing them from the person who should love you the most—leaves a hole in your soul that no one else can fill.

I should tell her that I'm sorry I stayed away for so long. I should tell her that I loved her. I try telling her now, but the words refuse to come. They are lodged deep inside my heart, and I can't get them out. I. Just. Can't.

I've always found goodbyes too hard to bear.

And this one...

This one...

21

Julie Martin, the homecare worker I met on my second day on the island, enters the room to find me sitting beside Mom.

"Who should we call?"

"Call?"

"A funeral home?"

I totally blank on the name. There are so few of them in town, I don't know how that's possible. Julie remembers it though. She calls them on her cell phone while a nurse arrives.

There's a raft of paperwork to fill out. She walks me through it. I sign my name a hundred times, and then it's time to go.

I stand on shaky legs and gaze down at my mother for the last time. We were never an affectionate family, but I stretch out my trembling fingers to brush the hair away from her forehead and bend to kiss her cheek. Her skin is cool beneath my lips, and I turn away from the bed.

Stephen is waiting where I left him. In the few hours since he pulled the car to a halt on the side of the highway, I've aged a thousand years. The nurse hands me a bag.

"Your mother's things."

The most I can manage is a nod as I trail aimlessly down the hallway toward the front entrance. Numb.

"I'll drive you home," Stephen says quietly.

"I can do it, Doc," Rob says.

He's standing behind Stephen. I don't know why he's here or how he's heard, but suddenly I am grateful for the efficiency of the small-town hotline. He tells me how sorry he is, and we lapse into a prolonged silence as he steers the car along the windy back roads.

IT GOES on like that for days. The waking, the eating, the planning, in a trance. I choose a simple casket, a simple service, all the while trying to imagine what my mother would have wanted. It's a futile endeavor. I barely knew her. For all I know, she could want a Viking funeral, complete with a barge and fire.

Until this moment, I never appreciated how a community bands together to help those in need. A few hours after I leave the hospital, the church ladies show up bearing dozens of plastic containers filled with a smorgasbord of food. As good as it smells, though, I can't bring myself to eat it. Even the neighbor, Jim, brings over baked beans. I stand with the refrigerator door open and add it to the plentifully stocked shelves.

Folks from all over the island attend the funeral. My mother was never a social butterfly, but I must not be remembering that right. The church is packed. Leigh greets me at the door with a hug, and together, we walk inside.

"My mother knew all these people?" I mutter into Leigh's ear.

"They're not just here for your mother, Austin. They're here for you too. You're one of us."

I'm still trying to absorb this as I spot Carley rushing toward me. Leigh places herself between us, warding Carley off with a stern look that stops her cold. I sit in the front row with Rob and his family on one side and Leigh and Blake on the other. Blake hasn't uttered a word since we arrived, while Leigh hasn't left my side. I'm thankful not to be sitting alone as the minster welcomes us.

"We're here to bid farewell to one of our own. Linda Martell grew up on this island. Many of us knew her as a caring neighbor and faithful friend. Linda was always quick to offer help to families in need—whether it was organizing our Christmas food drive or the Easter egg hunt for the children."

I don't remember my mother doing any of this when we were growing up. It's like he's talking about a different person.

The rituals of the funeral, the shaking of hands, the singing of hymns, reciting the psalms, I do on autopilot—pushing my grief below the surface, surprised by how deep it goes.

Leigh offers to ride in the limo with me on the way to the cemetery, but this is the one offer I decline. I've held it together pretty well to this point, but the cemetery...

I haven't been there since the day we buried Scott. Well, not Scott. An empty casket buried in the ground beside my father's headstone. Both of them lie somewhere beneath the waves. There are ghosts here I have no wish to confront. The pain of losing Mom opens a fresh tear in my soul. The limousine stops, and for the life of me, I can't bring myself to open the door.

A trickle of mourners streams past the car on their way to the gravesite. More than a few heads crane toward the limo as they stroll by. They can't see me through the tinted glass, but I'm sure they know I'm in here. They're waiting for me, but I'm hiding. Like a coward. Wishing I was anywhere else.

I look beyond the rows of headstones into a grove of evergreen trees. I see a movement in the shadows. Two people. A man and a woman stand in the shade of the swaying pines. The woman is facing away. She's angry. I can tell by the way she's standing—spine rigid, hands on her hips.

She shifts her position and I pull in a quick breath when I see who she's with. Blake.

He grabs her shoulders, like he's trying to shake some sense into her. She wrenches away. She heads down the hill toward the gravesite and I can see her face. It's Carley.

What is Blake doing out here? With her? And where's Leigh? I spot Leigh's blonde ponytail in the gathering of mourners by the graveside. She's standing beside Stephen.

I wonder if she knows where her husband is—who he's been talking to... Probably not.

Get moving.

It's my mother's voice that goads me from the limo out into the fall sunshine. I stand beside the grave and direct my gaze beyond the casket to a spot on the horizon, where the amber light of the waning sun casts its warm glow across a grove of deep green cedar trees, and pretend I'm there—somewhere safe. Beyond all this.

The minister's words are lost in the wind, and as the crowd thins, I linger. I place my hand on the casket one last time in a final farewell gesture. The cool wood slides beneath my palm. I turn to go.

My heart is heavy. A cloud of grief closes in as I trudge back toward the limo and retreat into the silence of the back seat. Alone. I ask the driver to drop me off at my mother's house and by the time he stops the car, I'm almost too drained to move. I climb out of the back seat and enter the house.

I don't see Cato stalk into the kitchen, but I feel him brush against my leg. He lets out a yowl. A full tin of Fancy Feast sits open on the countertop, exactly where I left it.

"Not hungry, buddy? I know just how you feel."

I scoop the cat up in my arms, half expecting him to claw me to shreds. But he doesn't. For once, he seems content. His fur is soft, and warm, and I scratch behind his ears. I hear the slam of a car door outside. I don't want to talk to anyone right now. I just want to be alone.

I head out the back door with Cato still in my arms and sit in the shade of the maple. Sunlight floats through the graceful canopy of leaves and warms my skin. The long grass hisses in the breeze. Cato grows restless and I let him go.

I don't know how long I've sat out here, but the sun has shifted and is fading to the west when I hear footsteps.

"Austin?"

A little start of surprise jolts me when I realize who it is. *Ellie.*

"How did you know I was out here?"

"Your car is out front. The door is unlocked. Your suit jacket is in the kitchen, along with your wallet and keys. I figured you couldn't be far."

I shoot her a lopsided grin. "You'd make one hell of a cop."

"So I've been told."

She doesn't ask if she can sit, she just does. She settles down beside me in the long grass and rests her back against the tree. After a while, she reaches out and takes my hand. Our fingers lace together, and something inside me shifts—cracks open—and the words I never meant to say come pouring out.

"I loved her, and I hated her. I know that sounds awful."

"It's not awful. It's sad."

"But aren't children supposed to love their parents no matter what?"

Ellie doesn't answer right away. There is grace in her silence. At last, she speaks.

"What you feel isn't right or wrong—it just is."

Tears sting my eyes, and I try to push them back, the way I've done countless times before, but I can't. I'm too tired. Too broken. They streak down my cheeks in a rush. I pull my hand from Ellie's and hide my face.

"It's okay," she says.

It takes me a while to regain control. I can't look at her. I wipe my eyes and clear my throat.

"You know what she said to me the morning of Scott's funeral?"

Ellie doesn't answer. I feel her comforting presence beside me, listening. "She said, 'Why couldn't it have been you?'"

A bitter laugh is ripped from the center of my being, and I shake my head. Even now, the words slash deep, opening a wound in my soul.

I know what Ellie's going to say. She didn't mean it. She was out of her mind with grief. We both were. But I knew the truth—if my mother could have met up with the grim reaper and made a trade, my life for his, she would have done so. In a heartbeat. She would have saved Scott and damned me to a watery grave along with my father.

"Oh, Austin."

The heat of Ellie's palm bleeds through the back of my shirt as she runs her hand across my shoulders. It's a sweet gesture. Comforting.

"That's why you never came back," she says.

I nod. "I never got over it. I never forgave her, and now—"

My memories feel like a heavy burden. I'm so tired. I don't want to carry them with me, away from the island, back to New York. I want to let all these feelings go, but for the life of me, I don't know how.

I sigh and tilt my face toward the warm sunshine. I listen to the birds, and the wind whispering through the trees.

"I've never told anyone that before. Not even my shrink."

"Wait, you have a shrink?"

She's joking, and I love her for it.

"Had a shrink. He fired me. He knew I was a lost cause."

"Not so lost, I think."

I turn toward Ellie. The sunshine lights the flecks of gold in her eyes, and I think that I've never met anyone quite so beautiful. A stray strand of hair floats across her cheek. She tucks it behind her ear, and I want to do that. I want to slide my hand across her cheek and feel the smoothness of her skin. I want to wrap my arms around her and never let her go.

The intensity of the feeling—primal and deep—startles me, and I turn away.

"When was the last time you ate?" she asks.

"Before the earth's crust cooled," I joke. It's not my A-list material.

"Come on, let's see what the church ladies brought you."

"The church ladies? God, you locals do know everything."

She rises from the grass with a laugh and offers me her hands. I take them.

"This is the second time you've rescued me."

Ellie's about to respond when someone calls out, "Austin, darling, there you are."

I stifle a groan. It's Carley striding through the hip-deep grass toward us.

Ellie drops my hands. Carley barges in between us and wraps her arms around me. She plants a kiss on my cheek and squeezes me tight. Too shocked for words, I stare helplessly over her shoulder, at Ellie, who averts her gaze.

"You poor darling," Carley cries.

I attempt to disentangle myself from her embrace, but it's too late. The damage has been done.

"I should be going," Ellie says.

Dammit. I don't want her to leave, but from the look on her face, I can tell that nothing I'm going to say will change her mind. I wipe the lipstick from my cheek, a passion pink brand that I can't get off soon enough as I watch Ellie go.

I need to fix this.

"I was at the church, but with Leigh standing guard, I couldn't get anywhere near you."

She takes a step toward me and instinctively I feint back. Her smile wilts a fraction.

In New York, girls intuitively know that one night doesn't mean forever. They slide on their stiletto pumps and are gone without a word, no guilt necessary, no speech—it's all nice and neat and simple. Clean.

But with Carley, nothing's simple. The world works differently here, and I screwed up, big time. And now I'm going to have to tell her so. I rake my hands through my hair and try to come up with the right thing to say, but coherent thoughts escape me.

"Look Carley...you and me...it's not going to work out."

Her jaw drops open. She looks shocked—as if she's been slapped.

"You're dumping me? Just like that?"

"Dumping you? We were never together."

Her lips contort into a grimace. Her eyes bore into mine. "Never together? What do you call what happened between us the other night? That meant something to me. You felt something too. You know you did."

Nothing I can say will make her understand, so I say nothing. An awkward silence stretches between us and I wish I could sink into the ground.

"It's her, isn't it?"

"Who?"

"Do you think I'm stupid? Her. Chief Sharpe."

"It's not about Ellie."

It's not just about Ellie.

Even to me, it sounds like a lie, and I can see the anger surface in Carley's eyes.

"You Martell boys are the same. You get what you want, and you don't care who gets hurt. If you think you're going to get away with this—"

Her hand connects with my cheek so hard, my fillings rattle. Blood fills my mouth and it's my turn to gape in shock as she pivots on her heel and marches away.

22

After Carley makes her grand departure, I head straight into the kitchen. I forage in the fridge and heap my plate full of Jim's baked beans, Mrs. Newman's lasagna, and a smattering of other local delicacies delivered by the church ladies. They don't call it comfort food for nothing. I even plow down a couple of date squares before I'm so full I can't move. I feel sick.

Stop when you hit Corning ware.

It's what my mother used to always say when I went back for seconds. Scott could be on thirds and she wouldn't say a word to him, but she never missed a chance to comment on how much I ate.

I'm sitting on the kitchen floor amid the landslide of mail. Even Cato looks disgusted by all I've eaten. My fork clangs on the plate and I push it away.

"I know. I'll go for a run later."

He shoots me a withering look. We both know that it's a lie. The day has left me so drained that I can barely stand. I stagger down the hallway, pick my way through the debris littering Scott's floor, and collapse onto the bed fully clothed.

As soon as my head hits the pillow, my mind picks up speed. A vortex of sorrow threatens to suck me down into a morass of memories. But I refuse to go there. I slow down my spinning thoughts by focusing on the brief moments of peace I found this afternoon, sitting under the tree with Ellie. Remembering the way Ellie's fingers linked with mine. I feel a soothing calm wrap around me. Those moments, before Carley stormed in and destroyed everything, are the last things I think about before I drift off to sleep.

I awake to find Cato curled up beside me in a ball. The furry curve of his spine is pressed up against my arm. Scott's lumpy mattress is a paltry upgrade from the couch. There's a few inches more of space, but god, I miss my memory foam mattress, my espresso machine, all the creature comforts of my real life that seem so far away.

My gaze sweeps across the debris-ridden floor. The realization that I'm going to be the one who decides what to do with all the stuff in this house hits me anew. Maybe I should have let Diana come. Within an hour of her arrival, she would have devised an action plan. Within eight hours, I have no doubt that she'd have hired an army of people to divide and conquer the mess, while I...

I can't leave it to strangers to sort through my brother's room. Scott's things are sacred. They're the last pieces of evidence left on earth that prove that he lived. Photographs spilled from a shoebox on the bottom shelf of the bookcase beckon me. I slide from the bed and cross the room.

Kneeling on the scratchy carpet, I gather the photos. Each one makes my heart ache as I think about everything that has happened since these snapshots were taken. Scott's friends have grown up, gotten married. Leigh is weeks away from giving birth to his best friend's child. It's not right.

I place a handful of photos in the box. The shelf shifts. I cock my head at the hollow clang of wood against wood. It's as if the shelf is floating against the base of the bookcase. I wiggle the shelf. It lifts free. The dusty rectangular base of the bookshelf is the perfect hiding place.

Tattered envelopes, yellowed with age, addressed to Scott. Letters. I should feel guilty about snooping, but writers are notoriously nosy.

The pages are covered in a pretty, looping script. Unable to deny my curiosity, I scan them. Most are love letters from Leigh to my brother while he was in Pullman at college. Near the bottom of the stack I find three others. The handwriting on these is a slanting, spiky scrawl.

DEAR SCOTT,

I wish I could hate you. I wish I could rip your heart out, the way you have mine, but I can't do it. I still love you. Despite everything. Even though you've gone back to her. Even though I've done everything you've asked. I aborted the baby. Our baby.

I can't stop thinking about what might have been—how we might have been if only you'd given us another chance. I hear you're back with her.

They say time heals all wounds, but this one runs too deep. Every time I close my eyes, I see you. How we were. How we could have been. Blake is the only one who understands how I feel. He would. He brought me to the clinic that day, waited for me until things were over. Drove me home. It should have been you.

I will always love you, Scott. It's my curse.

Yours,

Carley

I DROP the letter to the floor, as if the very touch of it wounds me. *A baby? Scott forced Carley to get an abortion?* Of course he did. There is no way he could have mended his relationship with Leigh otherwise. Every time she saw Carley toting Scott's child around town, she'd remember his betrayal.

But still...it's not the kind of thing I would have thought he was capable of. And Blake... I thought that maybe Blake and Carley were hooking up, but after reading Carley's letter, it's clear that there is so much more I don't know about their relationship. About all of them —Blake, Carley, and Scott. Only Leigh seems like an open book.

I try to push those painful thoughts from my mind, but I can't. I remember what Rob told me—about Cameron seeing Scott's boat at the bottom of the Sound. Like Carley, I wish I could forget, but for better or worse, I need to know what Cameron saw.

ROB GIVES me directions to Cam's place, but this can't be right. I've been driving down the dirt road for a good fifteen minutes, and still nothing.

Finally, I see a gap in the trees that leads to a rugged driveway. At least I assume it's a driveway. Gravel growls and hisses beneath my tires as I scour the horizon for a glimpse of the cabin. The cabin turns out to be this gorgeous contemporary two-story A-Frame log house with a wide front porch and floor-to-ceiling windows that could be straight off the cover of *Outdoor Living Magazine*.

Given Cameron's proclivities, my writer's brain envisioned something along the lines of a tar-paper shack or a lean-to. With raccoons. Certainly not this.

I turn off the engine and climb out of the car, thinking maybe I'm at the wrong place. I double check the address. Why I think this is going to help me is beyond my comprehension. It's not like there are street signs or house numbers or any other kind of landmark that's even the slightest inclination that I'm in the right place. I look around, slightly desperate, hoping maybe there's a Disney movie talking squirrel around to give me directions.

"Mother fucker."

The epithet shatters the idyllic quiet with such belligerent vehemence I know without a doubt I'm in the right spot. I hear the heavy clang of boots against metal and look up.

Twenty feet in the air, I see a skinny dude in work boots standing on the pitched roof like it's a sidewalk. The slightest careless act would end in shattered death, but that doesn't seem to bother Cameron. His fisted hands propped against his hips, he pulls the cap from his head and sends it sailing to the ground.

"Mother fucking piece of shit."

Just looking at him way up there gives me a gut-wrenching sense of vertigo. He spins toward the ladder.

"Have I come at a bad time?" I call as he drops to the earth.

A smile splits his stitched-up face and he lets out a howl. "Well goddamn, if it isn't Austin Martell himself. I heard you were home. How the hell are ya?"

Three strides later, he's standing in front of me. I try not to wince as he grasps my hand in his iron grip.

"What in god's name are you doing up there?" I ask.

He jerks his gaze back toward the house and surreptitiously I wiggle my fingers in a desperate attempt to restore feeling to my aching digits.

"Ah, fucking thing. I'm installing a couple of solar panels on the roof."

"By yourself?"

The wild gesticulation of his hands is frustration personified, and he swears again. "Shouldn't be that hard but the wires are cut wrong. If I hook it up like that, it'll short out in the rain. It's going to take me days to fix. Can't risk blowing out an inverter. Goddamn piece of shit."

When it comes to machines, Cameron is an absolute genius. Easily the smartest kid in the class, he had limitless potential. Cameron could have flown on Mars, cured cancer, you name it, that boy could have done it. But school bored Cameron. Everything came so easily to him that he skipped school and still got straight A's. The rare times when he did manage to show up for homeroom, he spent much of the day with his buddies in the woods behind school smoking dope. Staring into his bloodshot eyes, it's clear that some things never change. Cameron is flying as high as Major Tom.

The wasted potential nearly killed his father, an honest to god rocket scientist, who retired from NASA early and relocated from Houston to the island when Cameron was a freshman.

"You get enough sun out here for solar?" I ask.

The sun may be shining today, but for the next nine months I envision gray skies and enough rain to keep Noah and an army of carpenters busy all winter long.

Cameron grins. "Yeah, everyone says that, but Germany gets ten percent less sunlight than we do here in the Northwest and they have installed over fifty percent of the world's solar photovoltaic panels. If it makes sense for them to invest in solar, it makes a whole hell of a lot more sense for us. Sure, we've got long, rainy winters here, but those long summer days sure rack up the solar hours. And with the government incentives, I'd be stupid not to do it."

Government incentives? I don't even know what a photovoltaic panel is, but I have no doubt his assertions about the virtues of solar energy are true. Cameron knows his shit.

"So, Austin, what brings you all the way out here?"

"Scott."

Cameron picks up the baseball cap he pitched off the roof. He smacks it against his dirty pant leg before settling it over his thick thatch of hair.

"Well, shit. Someone told you about my dive?"

"I wanted to hear it from you."

Cameron sighs and pivots toward the house, waving me to follow along. I do.

The thrift store furnishing doesn't detract from the cabin's beauty. Huge windows face the woods, bathing the room with filtered light.

"God, Cameron. This place," I say, genuinely in awe.

"Finished it last winter."

"You built this?" I emit a low whistle from between my teeth.

"I bought the land from Dad."

"How long did it take?"

"Two years, give or take."

Cameron saunters into the kitchen and pours three inches of clear liquid into glass tumblers. He nudges one toward me. Some people frown on drinking before five o'clock in the afternoon, some before lunch. I've never been encumbered by such formalities, and I pick the glass up and give it a sniff. It smells like lighter fluid.

"Did you make this yourself too?"

Cameron grins. "Go on. It won't kill ya, it only blinds ya."

I salute him with the rim and take a swallow. This shit burns all the way down my throat and I cough a little as my eyes tear up. Cameron's grin widens.

"It will put hair on your ass."

"Not exactly the look I was going for but—"

Holy shit this stuff burns. I sputter and set the glass down. Everything from my mouth to my gut is on fire. Cameron laughs and thumps my back. I wave him off and clear my throat.

"So, Scott," I croak and wipe my eyes.

"Right. Scott. There I was diving off the coast with a few friends. You know, out for the day, kicking around the sandy-bottomed straight looking for crabs, when we came upon it."

"Scott's boat?"

"Yeah." Cameron pauses and takes another gulp of the offending stuff. He squints at me and shoots me a half-sober look. "You sure you want to hear this?"

"Would I be here if I didn't?"

"Fair enough. There are a few wrecks near the reef a mile or two off Deception Bay, some of them quite old. But Scott knew these waters too well to get anywhere near them."

I don't want to hear this. I really don't. I reach for the glass and power down another gulp of the homemade formaldehyde.

It fights back. I choke it down.

"The wind flipped the boat," I say.

Cameron shakes his head, shaggy hair falling into his eyes. "It's always bothered me."

"Why?"

"Because Scott was such a goddamned good sailor."

"But he was drunk."

"God, man, we were all drunk. Scott still should have been able to get the sails down in time."

My heart sinks. This is it? Pure conjecture about Scott's sailing skills and how he should have known better. It doesn't help. Suddenly I'm regretting having come, trying to dig up a past that should stay buried like my mother.

Besides, if there was something odd about the way Scott's boat went down, surely someone would have realized it years ago. Not now. Not a decade and a half later. What I'm feeling must show up on my face because Cameron thumps my shoulder hard enough to dislocate it.

"I'm telling you, Austin, as soon as I saw it, I knew it was the boat Scott went down in. We were all out at the resort that night, drinking, laughing. You were there too, bussing tables or some such thing. I remember seeing him leave the dock with Blake. One last sail before summer was over, right?"

I nod, though it isn't a question, and Cameron goes on.

"We ran back up the hill. I drank beer in the back of Rob's truck. We talked about heading off to Boomer's to smoke some weed, but we decided to wait for Scott and Blake. Then the storm hit. Early Pineapple Express comes screaming over the mountains."

Cameron takes another hit of the homemade jet fuel and drags a hand across his lips.

"It looked like a ghost ship, cast on its side and covered in silt. Weeds already growing on it. I swam around it. I don't know what I was looking for. Maybe some clue as to what went wrong that night."

Cameron pauses and refills his glass. I stop myself from prompting him, because while part of me wants to know what he found, a bigger part of me dreads hearing words that will shatter the uneasy resolution I've reached in the years since Scott's death.

"They didn't hit anything. There was nothing wrong with the hull. Not a goddamned thing. The sails were long gone. The masthead is buried in the mud, so I couldn't see much of the rigging. Everything looked right until I saw the seacock."

"The seacock?"

"Yeah. It's a valve on the hull of a boat. I had to scrape some of the crap out of the way, but it was clearly open. That doesn't just happen unless someone opens it."

"You're saying that if the seacock is open, the boat will sink?" I ask, grasping for the truth behind Cameron's words.

For the first time since I arrived, Cameron looks stone cold sober.

"A boat that size, in those kinds of conditions, will sink. Fast."

"But Blake said…"

Cameron's lips stretch into a fierce smile. "Yeah, Blake said all kinds of things."

I'm drowning in the subtext of what Cameron isn't saying. The thought so unspeakable, I struggle for words.

"Is there any way to explain the open valve?"

Cameron shrugs. "In this situation, there's only one explanation."

I guzzle the jet fuel in my glass, cringing to the very last drop. Cameron fills up the glass to the brim. I gulp that one down too.

My head swims as the alcohol hits me hard and I try to grasp for some explanation that makes sense. If Cameron is right, then Blake lied. *About everything.*

I feel sick, as if I might vomit the whole contents of my stomach up in a single whoosh. I wish none of this had ever happened. I wish that I was still back in New York, happy in my ignorance.

"There must have been an investigation. Why didn't anyone check the validity of Blake's story?"

"They were best friends," he says, as if I need reminding.

Cameron drains his glass and slams it down on the countertop with a note of finality. My head spins.

I remember hearing that the Coast Guard fished Blake out of the water. Bruised and battered, he was in the hospital while they continued to search for my brother, but Scott's body was never recovered. He never came home.

"Did you tell the police what you saw?"

Cameron snorts and tosses his hands in the air. "What was the point? I mean, regardless of how it happened, Scott is still dead. Nothing is going to bring him back."

He's right. Nothing will bring Scott back. Still, as I make my way back to the car, I try calling Ellie. When she doesn't pick up, I leave her a message.

I'm way too antsy to sit around the house and wait for her to call me back. Instead, I go looking for Blake.

23

In Manhattan, trying to find someone you barely know would be like trying to search for a piece of sea glass on the beach, but on an island this size...well, let's just say that it doesn't take long to find Blake's oversized black pickup truck parked outside the local hardware store.

I've researched enough mysteries to know that the first rule of surveillance is to find a way to blend in. Pulling into the lot in Mother's Mustang would be akin to hanging a blinking "hey, look at me" sign around my neck, so I swapped cars with Rob. He seemed quite happy to spend the afternoon cruising around in the Mustang. He wasn't at all happy when I swiped his ball cap though. It smells like bacon grease and cigarettes. I cringe a little as I settle the brim low on my brow.

The seconds drag by as I watch the entrance for any sign of Blake, but the longer I wait here, the more I feel like a low-rent private investigator staking out a cheating spouse.

When Blake finally does emerge, a cellophane bag swinging by his side, nothing seems amiss. He walks straight to his truck and climbs in. The next stop on this riveting tour of my hometown is the bank, where Blake parks a half block down. He doesn't go inside. He waits on the sidewalk for an older lady to finish her transaction. Isn't he aware there's an etiquette he should follow in these situations?

He's standing way too close to the old gal, who keeps sneaking nervous glances over her shoulder, because having this big behemoth of a guy hulking behind her while she's pulling money out of her account is making her jumpy.

Blake ignores the dirty look she shoots him as he steps up to use the machine. The transaction takes a minute. Maybe less. He is on his way back to the truck when someone calls his name. Blake turns to greet him. The guy is wearing tight jeans and a purple polo shirt that looks like it may have fit him twenty pounds ago. Belly shaking, he jogs a few steps to catch up to Blake.

From here, I can't hear what they're saying, but it looks like a friendly exchange. I pull out my phone and snap a photo just in case. Maybe Rob knows who he is. I no sooner snap the shot than the two are shaking hands. I watch to see if there's something off about it—a subtle exchange of drugs or money. I don't see anything suspicious, but who knows. I might have missed it. Blake climbs back in the truck, and we're onto the next spot.

How do cops do this? Following someone around for hours on end is mind-numbingly dull. With the sun slanting in through the window, and the effects of Cameron's moonshine wearing off, I yawn and slump against the door. Blake parks the truck and slings a workout bag over his shoulder as he heads into a gym.

Seriously, does this guy ever work?

This time of day, most people are toiling away at their mundane jobs. But not Blake. Half an hour later, he's dripping with sweat as I watch him pummel the heavy bag with all he's got. An earthquake erupts from each ferocious thrust of his fist and sends the heavy bag flying.

My eyelids start to droop, and I straighten in my seat and shake my head in a desperate attempt to stay alert. It's then that I see her. A woman dressed in skintight spandex. Her chestnut curls swing behind her in a thick ponytail that hangs halfway down her back. It's Carley.

What is it with the two of them?

She runs a gloved hand across his back. Blake stops the heavy bag from swinging and turns toward her.

That's right. Carley told me that Blake was teaching her how to kickbox, and for the next forty-five minutes, I watch them go at it. Blake's not taking it easy on her. He levels her with a right cross that sends her staggering back. But Carley doesn't quit. She shakes off the blow and goes back in for more.

Though she is clearly outmatched, Blake doesn't get away completely unscathed, as Carley lands a few solid kicks to his kidneys before he knocks her to the ground. Once she's had enough, they strip off their gloves.

That's the last thing I remember before someone knocks on the window. It's Ellie.

I bolt awake at the sight of her and scramble to roll the window down.

"You okay?" she asks.

I flash a sheepish smile. "Yeah, guess I nodded off."

"Uh-huh. Nice car. Did you get tired of the Mustang?"

"It's Rob's."

"I know," she says.

"Of course you do. Small town cops know everything."

"Should I ask what you're doing here?"

"Shopping."

It's a lie. We both know it as she shoots me a skeptical gaze.

"All right, I was watching Blake."

"Because?"

"It's a long story."

Ellie cracks a smile. "I've got time."

I scan the street for any sign of Blake's truck, but it's long gone. There is no sign of Carley's car either, and while the street isn't busy, there are a handful of tourists and locals strolling down the hilly sidewalks. I frown. News travels fast on the small town grapevine, and I don't want Blake to know that I was tailing him.

"Not here."

"You know I love a good story. Where?"

"My place."

24

E llie's intrigued enough to follow me back to my mother's house. She parks the cruiser behind Rob's car. We're heading down the driveway side by side when I see it. Beside me, I feel Ellie tense. There's a paper stuck to the front door, fluttering in the breeze. Though neither of us says the word, we're both thinking the same thing.

It's another note, like the one left on my car. Ellie darts ahead of me in full investigation mode. A knife is driven through the top of the paper, pinning it to the door. *A knife.* I mean, holy overkill. My editor would have ruthlessly plucked that melodramatic detail from my manuscript as if it were a noxious weed.

Ellie cocks her head and turns her quizzical gaze on me.

"Is that your mother's knife?"

"Who knows? With all the crap my mother kept in there..."

I lean in to get a better look. It's not a page from a book. It's a photograph ripped from a newspaper. A tingle of shock races down my spine as I realize where it was taken. Ellie pulls on a pair of thin latex gloves and pins down the edges so we can get a better look.

"The photo was taken in Seattle the night of the symphony," I say. "See that?"

Though the newspaper photo has been torn in two, I can still see an elbow tucked into the crook of my arm.

"Daphne Hammer," Ellie says.

It's not a question, but I nod anyway.

"She was with me when *The Seattle Times* reporter took that shot."

"Well, shit," Ellie mutters.

She heads back to the cruiser for an evidence bag, then carefully wiggles the knife free from the door and drops it inside. The newspaper clipping is bagged too.

"Wait here."

Ellie stows the evidence in her car before entering the house. Ignoring her directive, I wait in the kitchen as she finishes her search.

"You don't think someone was in here, do you?"

She shrugs. "Impossible to tell."

There is no sign of Cato. Blake is all but forgotten as a strained silence stretches between us.

"I don't like this," she says. "You should change the locks."

"There's no point. I'm not going to be here much longer."

Two weeks ago, the idea of returning to New York would have filled me with giddy glee, but now, I feel an unexpected pang at the thought.

Ellie surveys the wreck of the kitchen with a grim expression on her face. "I don't think you should stay here tonight."

"You think I'm in danger?"

"You and your mother were both attacked by an intruder. Mark Hammer's dead. And there's a stalker leaving you notes."

"A stalker?" Despite the gravity of the situation, I'm grinning like an idiot. "Chief Sharpe, I do believe you're worried about me."

"Worried? Of course, I'm worried."

"So, what do you suggest?" I cock an eyebrow and await her response.

"Do you have someone you can stay with?"

"Like I stayed on your couch that night?"

Her brows crease in a slight frown. "I'm not sure that's a good idea."

"Greg wouldn't approve?"

"It's not that..."

"Then what is it, Ellie?"

The use of her name is deliberate, and for the first time, she looks flustered. The air feels suddenly charged with ion particles that are slowly pushing us together. And I can't help it. Ever since that moment in her kitchen, I have wanted to kiss her.

She looks up into my face. Flecks of gold glimmer in her cinnamon eyes and I don't know if the timing is right, but with Ellie, there may never be a right time. If I don't do it now, I might not get another chance.

I reach for her, sliding my hands around the nape of her neck, and press my lip to hers. Her mouth tastes sweet, like raspberries in the sun, and something inside me unfurls—like I've been waiting for this, waiting for her my whole life.

I push forward, deepening the kiss, trying to memorize everything about this moment. Her soft skin. Her lips. The silky tresses of ponytail tickling the back of my hand. The way she fits against me. The way my heart soars as she kisses me back.

The elation of the moment is short lived though, as Ellie's fingers curl around my wrists. Her grip tightens. She pulls away and presses my palms together.

An emotion I can't name blazes deep in her eyes.

I'm still trying to interpret what it means when she says, "I'm not one of your girls, Austin."

Her words hit me with the sudden force of a slap and something inside me freezes.

"What are you talking about?"

"You. Women. Daphne. Carley. Those are only the ones I know about. God knows who else you're stringing along in your orbit. Regardless of what you might think, I am not a one-night stand."

"I never presumed you were."

My voice is colder than I intend. But hell, I didn't ask for this.

"This isn't New York. Did you think I'd just fall into your arms like one of your desperate bimbos?"

"Bimbos?" The heat of anger rises in my chest. "It's not like that, Ellie..."

I struggle to remain calm, but she's not listening. Ellie's cheeks are flushed and she's vehemently shaking her head.

"Did you or did you not sleep with Carley?"

The bluntness of her question stops me. I don't answer. I don't have to. She already knows the truth. I can see it in her eyes.

"You may enjoy playing games, but..."

"Games? You think I'm playing games with you?"

"The only reason you're remotely interested is because you can't have me. I'm a plaything—a challenge, a way for you to pass the time while you hang out in this podunk town. You said it yourself. You're not going to be here much longer. You'll go to New York and forget all about this—me—while I'm left here..."

Ellie stops mid-sentence. She presses her hands to her flushed cheeks.

"Let me save us both the trouble."

God, I want to shake some sense into her. She doesn't know how I feel. She can't. I don't fully understand it myself. She's like no one I've ever met. She's strong. And smart.

And leaving...

The door slams and I hear the distant growl of a car engine reversing out of the driveway. I kick the trashcan. Pain explodes in my foot.

Fuck it. Fuck her.

I don't need her to lecture me on my shortcomings. I am well aware that I fall somewhere south of perfection.

There's got to be something to drink in here. I scour my mother's cupboards. The bottle of gin I find tucked behind a box of cornmeal is probably older than I am, but hell—beggars can't be choosers.

Foregoing a glass, I drink straight from the bottle, determined to forget all about Ellie. And her sucky attitude. And her ugly cop shoes. If she can't see what's staring her right in the face, then she deserves to end up like one of those crazy cat ladies with too many sweaters. Alone.

25

My head throbs. Mixing moonshine with gin isn't exactly a pro move, and like a loser, I've been parked out front of the police station for over an hour, waiting for Ellie to come outside.

Just my luck, when she finally emerges, she's not alone. Two muscle-bound pillars in uniform flank her. It's not what I was hoping for, but I can't wait. I have to talk to her. Now. Before I lose my nerve.

I climb out of the car. Ellie catches sight of me and stops.

"May I have a word, Chief Sharpe?"

Her rigid shoulders and stony expression tell me she'd rather be flayed, but the fact that I've confronted her in public leaves her little choice.

"Go ahead, I'll catch up."

The twin pillars do as they're told. Ellie stands with her arms crossed, her feet shoulder-width apart, like she's bracing for a blow.

"Last night..." I only manage to squeeze a few shaky words out before she holds up her hand.

"Nothing happened last night."

"We should talk about it."

"There's nothing to say."

"Ellie..."

Though I'm trying hard not to show it, I feel shaky inside, but Ellie refuses to give me an inch. She's about to brush me off, so I blurt out the next thing that comes to mind.

"I never did tell you why I was following Blake."

She shifts her stance slightly, and I know this is my chance.

"I went to see Cameron, and he told me about a diving trip he took this summer where he came upon Scott's boat."

The story comes pouring out of me. I tell her everything about the boat and the seacock, with as much detail as I can muster. All the time I'm watching her, trying to intuit what she thinks. Her expression is as hard as granite. A few beats of silence pass before she speaks.

"What do you think it means?"

"What if Scott's accident didn't happen the way we thought? What if it was...deliberate?"

Ellie doesn't have to tell me that the kind of weighty accusations I'm tossing around are the kind that could tear people's lives apart. I know. She knows it too.

"Why would someone want to kill your brother?"

"Why would Blake want to kill him, you mean?"

"You're saying if something happened, Blake was the one to do it. I suppose that if we're going to be lobbing accusations, we might as well be specific."

"It was just the two of them on that boat. Who else could it have been?"

"They were best friends, Austin."

"I know, but even back then, he was in love with Leigh."

"So you think...?" Ellie trails off.

I think about Leigh, and her baby, and the hell I could unwittingly unleash if my suppositions were made public. And maybe I'm crazy, but as much as I want to, as much as I wish I'd never heard this information, I can't forget what Cameron said.

Ellie's staring at me, hard, and god help me, I'm hoping to see some spark of emotion in her eyes, some hint that maybe she cares enough about what I'm saying...about me not to dismiss me out of hand, no matter how improbable it might sound.

"Do you know how Cameron spends eighty per cent of his waking hours?"

My heart sinks and I know I've lost. There's no point in playing dumb. I know exactly where she's heading. I beat her to the punch.

"Stoned."

"That's right. Stoned."

"That doesn't mean he didn't see something. He's scary smart and the way he told the story...I believe him."

We stand there, glaring at each other. Ellie's expression remains flat.

"Go inside. Talk to O'Brien. He'll follow up."

"Thanks for listening, Chief."

She winces at my sarcasm.

"Just doing my job," she snaps.

26

My mind is thrashing over the conversation with Ellie. I need to calm down, so I hike down the hill toward the water. The wind is blowing off the Sound with a mild ferocity that tells me that summer is over. As the first bite of fall sinks into me, I know that I've been here too long.

Christ. I wish I'd never come back. I wish Mom hadn't died. I wish Ellie...

I stop the painful thought before it can fully form.

I want to wake up in Manhattan believing that everything can go back to the way it was, but if there's one thing I've learned since returning to this godforsaken island, it's that burying the past does not work. After fifteen years of relative peace, I won't have a second more unless I stop running from the truth—from my feelings.

The sidewalk opens onto the pier that wraps around the Coupeville Wharf. My footfalls echo on the worn wood. The smell of saltwater and fish wafts up from the churning waves. I lean against the railing and gaze out at the vast blue expanse that stretches out to the horizon. The afternoon sunlight slants across the Sound, catching the rocky shores of Deception Bay and turning the boulders to burnished gold.

As much as I may want to, I can't leave—not yet. Not until I know what happened on that boat. I owe it to Scott. To Mom.

And then there's Ellie...

I don't know what to do about my feelings for Ellie. If there is anything I *can* do, given what she thinks about me.

But maybe there is something I can do to find out more about what happened aboard the *Dreamcatcher* the night my brother died.

I pull the cell phone out of my pocket and search my call history until I find what I'm looking for. I dial the number for the forensic accountant friend of mine who has been digging into Leigh's financial records.

"Craig Stiles." He speaks like a New Yorker, and my sudden longing for the city intensifies.

"Craig, it's Austin."

"Hey," he says, his voice brightening. At least someone's glad to hear from me. "Funny you should call. I'm sifting through your friend's files. I don't have anything yet, but I should soon."

"Thanks, Craig. I had a question. Do you know who insures the resort?"

I'm assuming the *Dreamcatcher* belonged to the resort. And while there is no guarantee that Leigh hasn't changed insurance companies, I'm willing to bet she didn't. There are only so many agencies on the island and Leigh's the kind of gal to support a local business.

"Uh, let's see..."

Papers rustle in the background as he thumbs through the records. I mouth a silent prayer.

"Yeah. Here it is." He lists off the name of the agency. "Do you need the address?"

"No, I'll find it. When I'm back in the city, drinks are on me."

"Doubles?"

"Hell, the sky's the limit. I owe you."

I thank Craig and hang up.

Coupeville is small. The entire town could fit within four Manhattan city blocks. The agency is tucked away on a side street. The door beeps as I enter the office.

"May I help you?"

A smile is the gold coin of social currency and I play mine for all it is worth. The serious-looking gal with her hair tied back in a brown bun does not smile back.

"I'm looking for information."

"What kind of information?"

"About an accident."

"Are you a customer?" she asks, her fingers poised above the keyboard.

"No, not exactly. Mind if I...?" I point to the chair across from hers. Ignoring the reluctant look she gives me, I sit.

"It's about a sailboat."

"Your sailboat?"

"Not exactly."

She's impervious to my boyish charms. I can tell by the somber look on her face.

"Maybe we should start again. I'm Austin Martell, and you are?"

"Bethany Wallace."

"Bethany."

I extend my hand toward her. She shakes it. Her fingers are as frigid as an ice queen's smile.

"Here's the thing, Bethany. My brother died in a sailing accident fifteen years ago. I've recently uncovered some new information about the accident and I'm wondering if the insurance company, your insurance company, ran an investigation."

"How would I know that?"

"The claim would have been filed by the owners of the Willows."

"The Willows?"

"The resort out on Deception Bay."

"Do you own the Willows?"

Damned privacy laws.

"No, it was owned by a couple named Walter and Sandy Hudson. It's now owned by Leigh Parsons. The boat was called the *Dream-catcher*."

My attempt to sound authoritative fails. Bethany sits silently, formulating her refusal, I suspect.

"I'm putting you in an awkward spot, I know."

"If you're not the client, I can't divulge information about a claim."

"I'm sorry if I'm making you uncomfortable, but I assure you, I'm not asking for any details. I just want to know if there was a claim filed for the *Dreamcatcher* in September 2003."

"Really, sir..."

"Austin."

"Mr. Martell, all information about a claim is protected by law."

"Please, Bethany..."

Her lips compress into a thin white line, and she gives her head a stubborn shake. Frustrated that I've hit another dead end, I choose another tack—my Hail Mary play.

"Is your manager in?"

"My...?" Bethany's cheeks flush bright red as if I've said something scandalous. "My uh...manager...died."

I feel a tingle of surprise and anticipation race through me as a flash of intuition strikes.

"Who was your manager?"

"Mark Hammer."

"How long has he been your manager?"

She shrugs. "Well, the way I understand it, he took the business over five or six years ago. That was before my time though."

"Thank you."

I can barely breathe as I leave the office. It's not what I was hoping for, but I have hit something fundamental. I'm heading toward Rob's car when I hear someone calling my name.

"Mr. Martell."

I turn to see a woman behind me. She's out of breath from sprinting up the hill. I turn to greet her with the same kind of practiced smile I use at book signings.

"Hi."

"I'm Peggy Jones. I work at the insurance agency and I couldn't help but overhear. I'm a big fan of your work."

"Thank you, Peggy. That's nice to hear."

"I'm not at liberty to tell you this, but..." Her voice drops to a whisper. I lean in close to hear. "The answer to your question is yes."

"Yes?"

"There was a claim filed."

My heart quickens at the news.

"Any chance you could get me a report?"

"I could lose my job."

"I understand, Peggy," I say, feeling the sting of disappointment. "I wouldn't want to do anything that might get you in trouble."

"Here's the thing," she says. "Usually boat accidents are thoroughly investigated, but this one..."

"This one wasn't?"

She shakes her head. "It was the kind of perfunctory report that wouldn't stand up to an audit. And there's something else."

"Yes?"

"That's where it gets weird. Apparently, the accident was investigated by our old boss, Mark Hammer."

27

B y the time I leave Peggy on the street, I've promised her copies of all my books. And my firstborn. Or maybe I just offered to name my firstborn after her, which would be awkward if he turned out to be a boy. Anyway, she looks as excited as I feel as I race toward Rob's car.

Ellie doesn't answer my calls, and when I finally break down and call the station, she's unavailable. I decline the offer to talk to another officer and hang up. I pace the house for hours, willing her to call me back. Even Cato's had enough of me when I head over to her place.

It's fully dark when I arrive, and Ellie's driveway is empty. Daisy's furious barking greets my knock, but Ellie doesn't answer. I sit on the steps, determined to wait. A cold wind comes off the Sound, and I shiver in the dark.

It's late when her headlights finally swing into the driveway. I wait until she's parked and out of her vehicle before I move. The security lights turn on. Startled by the unexpected movement, Ellie reaches for her gun. She catches sight of me and her shoulders slump.

"Sweet Jesus, Austin. Never sneak up on a cop like that."

"I'm not sneaking. I'm—"

She doesn't give me a chance to finish.

"This is not okay. I should arrest you for trespassing."

"I found out something today."

"Tell it to O'Brien."

"Dammit, Chief Sharpe, the least you could do is listen."

She squares her shoulders, balls her fists on her hips, and breathes out a heavy sigh.

"Mark Hammer was the insurance agent that investigated the boat accident that caused Scott's death."

"How do you know that?"

"I found out through the insurance agency."

"You saw the insurance claim yourself?"

"No, Peggy Jones told me about it."

"And she is?"

"She works at the insurance agency. She looked it up."

"So you're taking someone else's word—"

"What other choice do I have? I can't get a warrant to look at the records, but you can."

"On what grounds?"

"You're the cop. You figure it out. The insurance claim connects Mark Hammer and Blake to the boat Scott went down in. That's got to mean something."

"You can't make those kinds of assumptions—"

Frustration explodes inside me. I jab my finger toward Ellie's chest.

"Goddammit, it's all connected. All you have to do is find the missing piece. Who broke into my mother's house? What was he looking for? What happened on that boat? I'm begging you, Chief Sharpe, just do your fucking job. Or are you so afraid of your feelings for me that you refuse to work the case?"

Inside the house, Killer is barking like she wants to rip off my head. I leave Ellie gaping after me, still standing in the dark.

28

I park in my mother's driveway and slam the car door. Something brushes against my legs and I let out a yelp so loud I startle the cat. Cato's green eyes glare up at me, his luminous gaze filled with disdain.

"God, you scared the shit out of me," I say. "What are you doing outside?"

He trots toward the house, unrepentant. I follow in his wake. The deep silence is unnerving. A chill ripples down my spine. I feel as if I'm being watched. I search the deep shadows for some sign of movement, but it's so dark, I can't see a damned thing. I hurry inside.

As soon as we enter the kitchen, the cat lets out a yowl.

"Demanding beast, aren't you?"

He devours his tin of Fancy Feast while I open the refrigerator door, looking for Mrs. Newman's lasagna, when my stomach drops. There, on the top shelf, is a bottle of chilled champagne. Not just any champagne. Dom Perignon. The sight of it freezes me to the spot. It mirrors a scene at the beginning of the second act of *For Love or Money*.

My hand trembles as I slam the door shut. My appetite has fled, and I know I should call the cops, but after the whole scene with Ellie tonight, I can't. I'll deal with it in the morning.

I check to make sure the windows are closed and the doors are locked before I head down the hall, where Scott's bed awaits. With the tornado of shit whirling around inside my head, I figure that sleep is going to be damned near impossible, but no sooner does my head hit the pillow when I'm out.

The far-off sound of sirens penetrates my consciousness. I breathe in a deep breath. Christ, it's hot. The air conditioning must have kicked out.

I roll over in bed and throw off the covers. My outstretched hand hits the wall. And that's when I know. I'm not in my bed, in my condo, or my city. I'm here. In my mother's house.

And something isn't right.

Smoke.

I shake off the layers of sleep. Inhale. A stab of fear slashes through me.

I leap out of bed and lurch into the hallway. The alarm blares through the din of the fire. Black smoke fills the corridor. Burns my eyes. I bury my nose in the crook of my arm and stumble for the nearest door. *The kitchen.*

A furnace blast of heat hits me. Drives me back the way I came. I'm coughing. Running. Panicked. I race toward the largest window at the back of the house. In my mother's room. Something furry streaks past my bare legs. I scoop him up. Cato.

Orange flames lick the ceiling as I drive my shoulder into the bedroom door. Wood shatters as it slams against the wall. Cato's claws tear at my forearms. He's fighting, clawing to get free, but I refuse to let go.

I grab a chair tucked in beside my mother's dresser and heave it toward the window. The force of the collision jolts up my arm. The glass cracks. Shatters. I toss the chair through.

I launch Cato through the gaping hole into the black night. The howl of the fire closes in. Wood sizzles and pops as the dying house goes up in flames. The heat of it sears my skin.

I brace my palms on the window pane and leap outside. Hot ribbons of pain shoot through my hands as the glass shreds my flesh.

I land in the tangled, overgrown mass of hydrangea bushes beneath my mother's window. Scratched, bruised, and bleeding, I struggle to my feet.

A coughing spasm hits. I crumple in the cool grass beside the laurel hedges and watch in horror as the roof gives way. Bright orange sparks fly out in all directions.

"Cato," I sputter.

But the cat's nowhere to be found. I call again and double over as another coughing fit takes hold. A high-pitched sound cuts through the roar of the raging fire. Sirens. Honest-to-god sirens come roaring down the blacktop toward the burning house.

The cool wind dries the sweat on my skin, and I shiver. Just then, something warm drops around my shoulders. A blanket. I look up. It's the neighbor, Jim. He's in his boxer shorts. His belly strains against a stained white undershirt stretched across his midriff.

"You okay, son?"

I'm not really, but I nod anyway. He pats my shoulder.

Flashing red lights slice through the darkness and I struggle to my feet. My hands are sticky with blood as I pull the blanket tight.

The fire truck screeches to a halt at the end of the driveway. Firemen teem like ants from the bright red engine and race toward the flames. Hoses are uncoiled. Orders are barked as the firemen get to work. One of the men hurries over to where Jim and I stand.

I think it's a man, but I'm wrong; it's a woman's face looking back at me.

"Anyone inside?" she yells.

I shake my head. A white, foamy spray battles the orange flames. I stare on in impotent horror at my childhood home.

Neighbors shuffle down the road and huddle on the gravel shoulder. They stand together, watching in numbed shock as the destruction unfolds. I don't hear the police arrive. It isn't until Ellie is standing in front of me, shaking me, that I realize they're here.

Gone is the frigid indifference I saw in her face only hours before.

"Austin, what happened?"

"I don't know. I was sleeping and I heard..."

"The smoke alarm?"

I'm coughing too hard to speak. I nod instead. She catches sight of my tattered hands clutching the blanket.

"You're bleeding."

"What?"

I flex my hands open. Pain flares like a thousand bee stings and I hiss. Ellie takes my hands in hers and examines the cuts. Blood is caked in the thick gashes crisscrossing my palms.

"Okay, tough guy, I suppose you're going to tell me it's just a flesh wound."

"That's a cop line," I say, with the ghost of a grin.

I'd love to pretend that I'm that tough, but the cuts hurt like a... well...you know... Ellie is still cradling my hands. All the anger I felt this afternoon has melted away.

"I'm taking you to the hospital."

"I should stay."

"There's nothing you can do here."

She lets go, and I turn my gaze back to the fire.

Everything that once belonged to my family was in that house. Scott's trophies. My laptop. All gone. The full impact of the loss hits me, and I huff out a breath like I've been punched in the gut. Ellie eyes me with concern.

"You're sure you're okay?"

Whatever I am, it is definitely not okay. There are no words to describe how I feel. Devastated? Shaken? Bereft? These words pale compared to the emotional tsunami crashing over me. I meet Ellie's gaze.

"Let's stop at the station and grab you some sweats."

I shoot her a confused look. She answers with a wry grin. Her gaze drops to the gap in the blanket loosely folded around me.

"I've seen the whole show before. Well, almost the whole show. You don't want to give the nurses something to gossip about. Being a local celebrity, you have a reputation to uphold."

I love her for mocking me.

"Can't have that," I mumble.

I gather the blanket around my shoulders and buckle the seatbelt. Ellie slides behind the wheel and loops the car back toward the highway. There is no traffic this time of night. The silence that falls between us is punctuated by the gruff bursts of cop speak. Ellie radios in her location, but I'm not listening. My thoughts are far away.

"Any idea what could have happened?"

I shrug. "I told Stephen the house was trying to kill me."

She doesn't laugh at the joke.

"It's an old house," she says. "Once the fire investigators get a chance to sift through the damage, we'll know more."

I don't respond. If it weren't for all the crazy shit I'd uncovered in the past few days, the idea that it might be arson would have never entered my mind. But now, it's impossible to ignore.

"The Hammer's dead. My mother's dead. Someone broke into the house. Twice. No. Three times. That we know of."

"Three?"

I tell her about the champagne bottle in the refrigerator and wait for her to comment, but she doesn't. She doesn't have to. I know she's smart. I know that whether she's ready to admit to it or not, she's lined the evidence up like pearls on a string the same way I have.

Ellie pulls into the police station and tells me to wait in her office while she retrieves a set of sweats. She returns a few minutes later and she hands me the folded clothes. Our hands touch. Ellie shivers. The movement is slight, but I catch it. Maybe she's not as indifferent to me as she lets on.

"Look, Austin..." she says, her voice strained with emotion.

The next move is hers. I want her to say something, to close the distance between us, but she doesn't. She shakes her head, like she's fighting herself. I know exactly how she feels. I want to touch her, but after everything that has happened between us in the last twenty-four hours, I don't dare.

"I'm glad you're not hurt."

"That's not what you were going to say."

Her gaze lingers on my soot-streaked face. She touches my arm, and for a brief second, I feel her resolve waver. Then her hand falls away and she turns. I hear the door close as I release my breath.

29

Ellie's waiting outside the examination room when I emerge.

"The doctor says I'm going to be fine. As fine as I'm capable of being...you know..."

I finish with a shrug, but Ellie doesn't laugh. She doesn't even smile.

"It's not funny."

"I know."

Professional courtesy or not, I like that she's worried about me. She's teetering on the edge of exhaustion, and I should shoo her out of here, but I'm not ready for her to leave.

"Austin..."

The wariness in her gaze kills me. I want her to look at me the way she did that morning in her kitchen—before I kissed her. Before she threw Carley in my face. It's agonizing to want what you can't have. Everything inside me yearns for Ellie. We're standing a foot apart, but she might as well be three thousand miles away.

"Where will you go?" she asks.

"The doctor says I can crash here for the night. There's an empty room down that hall."

"And after that?"

I shrug. Raise my palms. "Rob's maybe."

"Maybe you should go home, Austin."

To New York? How I wish I could.

"Sorry, Chief. You're not getting rid of me that easily."

"Solving the case is my problem," she says. "Let me take care of it." There's a hard edge to her voice, and I know she means it. Ellie's a bulldog. "I'm not kidding, Austin."

"I know."

A spark of frustration blazes in her cinnamon eyes. My fingers itch with the need to touch her. I want to bury my hands in her hair and kiss her until she forgets all the stupid things I've done and said. But I don't. I head down the hall toward the empty room.

"Stay away from Blake," Ellie calls.

I raise a hand, acknowledging the comment, and turn into the empty room.

HOURS LATER, I fall into a restless sleep, only to jar awake when I hear Stephen's wry tone.

"Well, look what the cat dragged in," he says.

"Christ, what a night."

"So, I heard. Seems you have karma to burn."

"Burn. Funny. You missed your calling. You should have been a comedian," I say.

The thin hospital mattress is only marginally more comfortable than Scott's bed. I don't know which of us groans louder, me or the bed, as I hit the button and shift it into a sitting position.

"You look like hell. Let me check you out."

"Your esteemed colleague has already had the pleasure."

Stephen insists on giving me the once over and I'm too tired to argue.

"You may have burned one of your nine lives, but all things considered, you didn't fare too badly. How are your hands?"

"I won't be performing surgery anytime soon."

Stephen laughs. "We're all grateful for that."

In truth, they hurt like a sonofabitch, but I don't tell him. I'm due to take some Advil soon, and though I know it wouldn't take much arm twisting to get something stronger, I resist. I need to keep my wits about me. While Ellie would like nothing better than to see me sit by while the slow wheels of justice turn, I have other plans.

"Need a place to stay?"

The offer takes me by surprise.

"That's generous of you, but—"

"Oh, you thought I meant with me? No," Stephen laughs. "There's a homeless shelter in Coupeville..."

"Funny," I smirk.

"Seriously, I have a guest room if you need it."

"I may take you up on it."

Satisfied that my life is no longer in imminent danger, Stephen continues on his rounds. I borrow Mrs. Newman's phone to call Diana. She's suitably horrified by my news.

"This is insane. I want you on the next plane to New York. I'm calling the airline now—"

"Calm down, Diana."

"Dammit, Austin, I will not. Someone burned down your house with you in it. I don't know what's going on in that fucked up little town of yours, but you need to get your ass back to New York before something worse happens."

It takes a good fifteen minutes to talk Diana down. Finally, she agrees to wire me some funds to tide me over while I contact my bank and start the arduous process of replacing my ID.

After stopping by a local bank to pick up the wired funds, I go shopping at the Star Store to pick up some basics. A few changes of clothes. Socks. Underwear. Toiletries. Enough to see me though the next few days. I even pick up a new cell phone. The pay-as-you-go kind one of my characters would call a burner phone.

I pay for the goods and then head up the hill toward the Willows. With every step, I can hear Ellie warning me to stay away from Blake.

But if I'm going to find out what happened to my brother, I have no other choice.

30

Angry clouds bruise the sky. Teardrops of rain roll down my newly purchased Gortex coat as I trudge toward the Willows. The weather forecast says that the storm will break by morning, but the way it's looking now, the worst is yet to come.

I climb the stairs onto the porch and skim off my hood. I stop at the desk to book a room. The clerk's accusing stare shifts from me to the pile of cash sitting on the countertop.

"I need to see your ID. It's policy."

Just my luck, I get the one person on the island who doesn't know who I am.

I know Leigh would vouch for me, but she's nowhere in sight. Thank god the small lending library beside the fireplace has one of my books. I grab it from the shelf and plop it down on the countertop face down. There's an author photo on the back.

"That's me. Austin Martell."

The clerk's eyebrows arch. Her gaze shifts from the photo to my face and back again. Okay, to be fair, I'm looking a little rough. My black eye is fading. The cut on my forehead is healing, and though I washed up in the hospital, I still smell like smoke. No wonder she's having trouble buying it. The guy on the back of the cover looks like the worst thing that's ever happened to him is to run out of martini olives, while I...

Thankfully, one of the wait staff from the bar drifts through the lobby and shoots me a friendly wave.

"Hey, Austin."

And that does it. While the clerk types my info in the computer, I flip through the book. There are no missing pages. She hands me a room key and I depart.

On my way toward the stairs, I spy a tiny closet of a room they call a business office and duck inside. The ancient computer on the floor looks a mere generation or two away from its mainframe ancestors. Despite its prehistoric age, it's a portal to the outside world, and now that my laptop has gone up in flames, it's the best I've got. The hard drive wheezes as I launch the web browser and log into my email account.

I scan through the backlog of messages when I see it—a message from my accountant friend, Craig. I double click.

Give me a call when you get a chance.

Though the tone of the email isn't urgent, my curiosity is piqued. I program Craig's number into my new phone before heading upstairs.

While the room isn't New York posh, the Northwest décor is starting to grow on me—white walls with accents of cedar and slate. Compared to Scott's battered twin, the king-sized mattress is as soft as a cloud. I sink into it with a grateful sigh.

I'm intending to close my eyes for a minute or two before calling Craig, but sleep overtakes me. It's just after seven o'clock and fully dark when the sound of a door slamming down the hall wakes me.

I rise from the bed. The faint smell of smoke still clings to my skin like sweat, and even the scaled-back Whidbey Island version of myself can't justify going anywhere looking like this. I arrange the toiletries I purchased earlier on the countertop beside the sink and head to the shower. Minutes later I emerge, still looking like hell. The neatly trimmed beard I arrived with is starting to resemble the scruffy pirate version Rob wears. I go to work.

I've worn a beard for so long that even I can't remember what I look like without it. I run my hand across my freshly shaven jaw, shocked by what I see. A shiver rattles down my spine. It's like seeing a ghost. Without the beard, I look freakishly like Scott.

I turn away from my reflection. My grumbling stomach reminds me that it's time to eat. I cross the room to retrieve the car key and see the phone.

Craig. Right.

I calculate the time difference as the line connects. Craig answers.

"Hey, sorry for calling so late. It's Austin. What's up?"

Driven on by my rumbling stomach, I leave the room and head down the hall.

"Glad you called. I was going to send an email but..."

"But?"

He hesitates. "It wasn't the kind of thing I wanted to put into writing. Not without talking to you first."

A surge of surprise brings me to a halt on the landing at the top of the stairs. From here, I have an unobstructed view of the lobby. I spy Leigh leaving the dining room closely followed by Blake. The way her hands slash through the air in sharp, rapid gestures, I can tell they're arguing. He grabs her wrist. My gut clenches.

And for a second, I have forgotten all about Craig.

"Austin. You still there?"

"Yeah. Sorry. Go on."

"Someone has been skimming money from the business," Craig says.

Oh, shit.

"For how long?"

"Years."

"How much money are we talking?"

"Several thousand a month. Cash withdrawals. On its own, it's not a ton of money, but over time, it adds up. It certainly explains their cash flow problem."

"Who?" I ask, although part of me already knows what he's going to say.

"Someone with signing authority on the account. One of the owners, I'd guess. The withdrawals stopped a few months back."

"You're sure about this?"

"Positive. It's all here. I can send you the details."

"And the other thing I asked you to look into?"

"See, that's where it gets interesting. Your friend, Mark Hammer, had a river of dirty money flowing into his account."

"From where?"

"Cash deposits. Nothing huge. A few hundred here, a couple of thousand there. But here's the interesting thing: Some of those cash deposits match the withdrawals from the Willows account. Same amounts. Same dates."

Extortion.

We both know that he didn't get Hammer's info through appropriate channels, but it doesn't matter. Ellie has access to his financial records. She'll be able to connect the dots, the same way that Craig did.

"I need you to send the local authorities what you have on the Willows. Tonight."

I give him Ellie's contact info and Craig agrees.

"You've been a big help, Craig. I owe you."

"Name a character after me in your next book."

I promise to do just that. I shove the phone in my pocket and by the time I reach the main floor, Blake is gone. My fingers curl into fists as I march toward Leigh.

"Where is he?"

Startled by the expression on my face, she falls back a step.

"Who?"

"Blake."

"At the dock. Austin, what's wrong?"

I am going to make him hurt.

31

Without answering Leigh, I head outside. Icy drops of rain slash down from the charcoal sky, but I barely feel them. The fury building inside me eclipses everything. The sound of Leigh calling to me. The wind. The deep growling thunder that rolls across the bay.

The stairs that lead down the rugged hillside to the dock are on the other side of the parking lot. I jog toward them. Blake is down there. He killed my brother. I have never been more certain of anything in my life. I want to rip that bastard apart with my bare hands.

Yellow cones of light from the lampposts overhead punctuate the darkness. He's a shadow at the end of the dock moving between the boats.

The clang and thump of the hulls slamming against the pier masks my footsteps as I stride toward him. Whitecaps batter the edge of the dock. Blake is hunkered over the mooring, securing the last boat on the end.

My footsteps reverberate on the wooden surface. Startled, Blake looks up.

A crack of lightning splits the sky. The flash of light illuminates him. The shock that ripples across his features is quickly replaced by fear.

He scrabbles back a step. Mouths a name.

Scott.

A vicious grin contorts my face. I don't wait for him to stand. I cock my fist and drive it into his temple, putting my weight behind the blow. My knuckles collide with bone. The force of the punch splits my skin.

"What happened on that boat?" I scream.

We both know there's more than one version of the truth—the lies we tell ourselves so many times that we almost believe it. Then there's the other kind—the darker version of events we can't allow ourselves to speak.

Blake blocks the next blow. Fast as lightning, his foot shoots out and sweeps my legs from underneath me. I crash to the dock. Sparks of pain sear through my body. I clamber to my feet.

"What the fuck?" he yells. "The boat sank in the storm. I tried to save Scott—"

"You knew they were engaged. You were never going to have her."

"You're fucking crazy."

"You were his best friend."

Blake lunges at me like a charging bull. His size is a problem. He's bigger and stronger. Speed is my only hope. I dodge his charge. Grabbing his jacket, I pull him past me. Blake lands on his side.

"You've been paying Hammer off for years because he knew you lied. You sank that boat to cover up what you had done."

I drive my foot into his gut. Blake grunts.

"You killed him because you wanted Leigh."

"She deserved better."

"She deserves the truth."

He grabs my ankle. Twists. Jerked off balance, I careen sideways and land on the edge of the dock. The metal cleat drives into my ribs with a ferocious spike of pain. Blake grabs my shoulder and shoves my head into the frigid, brackish water. I hold my breath and blindly grasp for his throat. I latch onto his windpipe. Squeeze. Blake lets go.

I pull my head out of the water and push away from the edge of the dock, coughing. Blake rears up like Godzilla and drives his fist toward my face. I jerk to the side. The blow pounds into the dock. Wood splinters. He screams. I roll away from him and struggle to my feet.

Another peal of thunder rolls across Deception Bay. Blake advances. I step back. I'm too close to the end of the dock. There is nowhere to go. I plant my feet. A flash of lightning arcs across the black sky. Blood sheets down the side of his face—a twisted mask of rage.

"I will not let you ruin everything I've built. My life. My family."

Blake lunges. His knuckles slam into my jaw in a bright explosion of pain. Coppery blood fills my mouth. I grab his hair. Yank. Pull him down. I drive my knee into his face. He stumbles, grabs hold of me. Takes me down with him. My head cracks against the dock. Blood and sweat sting my eyes.

He moves. Fast. Pins me beneath his body. His knee digs into my chest. I fight for breath beneath his crushing weight. It's no use. I can't breathe. Black spots crowd my vision. Panic thrashes inside my mind. He's going to kill me. Like he killed Scott. I know it.

Then I hear something. A scream. High-pitched. Jagged.

Leigh.

Blake's attention moves away from me. His weight shifts. I gather my strength and shove him off. He tumbles to his side. And I can breathe. Wet air fills my lungs in great shuddering breaths.

"You bastard," Leigh screams. "What did you do?"

Leigh's horrified gaze slides between Blake and me. Only it's not me she's seeing. It's Scott. The shock of the truth unfolds upon her stricken face. The sound of her anguished cry slashes through my heart.

"You killed him. Didn't you?"

"It was an accident."

"Don't lie to me."

Blake walks slowly toward her. Hands raised. Pleading. But she backs away.

"Get out of here, Leigh," I yell.

I don't want her, or her baby, anywhere near Blake. He's unpredictable. Dangerous. But she ignores my warning. She ducks around him and positions herself between us. Protecting me when she should be protecting her baby.

Blake snarls. He grabs her shoulders and yanks her toward the center of the dock. Her fists pummel his shoulders with small, ineffectual blows.

"Listen to me—"

"Let me go!"

My knees are rubber as I charge him. Blake doesn't hear me coming. I grab him from behind. My arm snakes around his thick neck and grips it tight. He releases Leigh.

His elbow jerks back, connecting with my solar plexus in a blinding flash of pain. I force myself to hold on as he spins. Blake rears back and slams me against a lamppost. The light above us breaks. Amber sparks rain down across the dock.

Winded, in pain, I can't hold on. I drop like a stone. And he's there. On me. Hammering my body with his violent blows. My arms curl around my head as I try to hold on.

"Step away from him, Blake!"

A tremor of hope fills me at the sound of Ellie's voice.

The breath scrapes in and out of my lungs. I'm on all fours. Blood mixes with the salty rain that streams down my face. Leigh runs to me. Her hands latch onto my shoulders.

"Austin? Are you okay?"

I hear a sound. A half-snort, half-sob from Blake, who is staring down at us with the look of a condemned man.

"Put your hands on your head, Blake," Ellie commands.

I see it. A flash of desperation. A slight shake of the head. I scream. Try to warn Ellie. But it's too late.

Blake whirls on her. Charges.

The sound of a gunshot splits the air. Blake freezes for an instant. Leigh shrieks as he crashes to the dock. I wrap my arms tight around

Leigh; my only thought is to keep her safe. She flails in my embrace, but I refuse to relinquish my grip.

Footsteps pound across the dock as the cops converge on Blake.

I am still holding onto Leigh when a voice says, "It's okay. You can let her go now."

I recognize the blond cop. Officer O'Brien. I do as he says. He helps Leigh to her feet. She's crying. Shaking. Relieved, I close my eyes. I can hear the voices around me. The rain patters against my face.

"Goddammit, Austin."

"Ellie."

She's there. Standing over me. And she looks pissed. Despite the pain, despite everything, I smile.

32

Ellie helps me to my feet. A wave of nausea rolls over me, and I fight to remain conscious. *Breathe through it,* I tell myself. When I open my eyes again, I see Blake—flat on his back. Immobile. I don't need to ask if he's dead. I already know.

"Can you walk?"

I have no idea, but I nod anyway.

"Where's Leigh?" I ask.

"On her way to the hospital."

Ellie guides me up the stairs. It's a slow walk. My ribs are killing me, and my head is throbbing when I reach the top. I pause at the landing to catch my breath. And though I know I shouldn't, I take one last look at the man who killed my brother.

It isn't justice. Nothing will bring Scott back. I feel no joy at Blake's death, but at least the woman my brother loved won't be spending the rest of her life with a murderer. With the truth exposed, maybe we can both find some peace.

An ambulance is waiting in the parking lot and Ellie guides me toward it.

"How did you know?" I ask.

"Your friend, Craig, sent me the file. As soon as I read it, I knew where you'd be—ignoring everything I said about staying away from Blake."

"Am I that predictable?"

She snorts. "You're about as crafty as a third grader."

"Ellie..."

Everything I want to say comes rushing to the surface. I want to tell her how I feel, but before I can get the words out, she's pulling away.

"You're in good hands with Nico here. I've got a scene to process."

"Yeah."

"Have a seat," Nico, the EMT, says.

I'm as weak as a toddler and in no shape to argue. A stab of light pierces my corneas as he shines a pen light into my eyes. Carefully, he raises my arms. A bolt of pain shoots through me as Nico prods my side.

And that's it.

Everything goes black.

I awake sometime later, at the hospital. Everything feels sluggish. I'm dimly aware of the pain, but it feels distant. Far away.

"And he's back."

It's Stephen. He stares down at me with a rueful grin and shakes his head.

"You never do anything halfway, do you? It appears you've used up another of those cat lives of yours."

I blink. Try to shake my head, but pain throbs behind my eyes at the slightest movement.

"Easy," he says. "You've got a concussion."

"No shit, Sherlock. I could have told you that."

"At least your sense of humor's intact," Stephen says. "Two cracked ribs. Ten stitches in your forehead. We did our best with the stitches, but you may end up with a scar."

"Chicks dig scars," I say.

"But glory lasts forever." Stephen grins, not missing a beat.

"*The Replacements.* Keanu Reeves."

"Warner Brothers released it in 2000," Stephen adds.

"How's Leigh?" I ask when our laughter fades.

Stephen's grin disappears.

"She went into early labor. The good news is that both mother and son are doing fine. She's a few rooms down. Resting."

IT TAKES a full twelve hours of convincing before Stephen agrees to let me visit Leigh, and only if I take a wheelchair. I finally sweet talk a nurse into wheeling me down to Leigh's room. It's after visiting hours. I pause outside the doorway, not wanting to intrude. I'm relieved to find that she's alone. Except for the bundle in her arms.

The tender look on Leigh's face is heartbreaking. Unexpected tears form in my eyes and I blink them away. Rap on the door.

Leigh looks exhausted. The color has drained from her face and dark circles shadow her red-rimmed eyes. And no wonder. She's been through hell. She beckons me inside. The nurse obliges.

"Five minutes," the nurse says as she sets the brakes on my wheelchair and leaves the room.

My gaze rests on the impossibly tiny baby asleep in Leigh's arms. She gives me a sad smile. Her eyes fill with tears.

"I'm so sorry, Leigh."

"I know. Me too."

"How is he?" I nod toward the sleeping bundle.

She pulls in a shaky breath. "Perfect. All ten fingers and toes."

"I'm glad. Where are your parents?"

"I sent them to the resort. I wanted some time to myself."

A tenuous silence falls between us. I want to brush her tears away, to tell her that it's going to be okay, but I don't. It sounds trite. I know what it feels like to lose a brother, but the pain that she must be feeling now, I can't presume to understand. The baby lets out a small cry but doesn't wake.

"He loved you, Leigh. They both did."

She blinks hard. I reach for the box of tissues. A spike of pain impales my ribs. I clench my teeth and hand her the box.

"I'm sorry," she says as she wipes her eyes, "about Scott..."

A lump of sadness forms in my throat. I slowly shake my head.

"You have nothing to be sorry for."

"I should have known."

"How could you? Blake had us all fooled. The important thing is that you're safe and you have this little guy."

She sniffs and gives me a nod.

"Would you like to hold him?"

I'm surprised to find that I would. I nod and hold out my hands. She passes me the baby and I gather him to my chest. His eyes open and he looks straight at me. I can't help it. I smile back.

"Well, hello there."

I'm doing that thing I see so many people do. I make disgustingly cute baby noises. He opens his mouth and lets out a yawn. I laugh.

"I know just how you feel, buddy."

There's something magical about holding a baby. I'm humbled by the absolute trust in his eyes. And like the Grinch, I feel my heart expand. In another life, this could have been my nephew. Scott would have liked having a son of his own to throw the football around with, to teach him how to sail.

"You know what I named him?"

"Austin, of course."

To my relief, Leigh smiles at the joke.

"Close. I named him Scott."

Overcome by the bittersweet moment, I'm unable to speak.

"He's going to need a godfather," Leigh says. "Do you think you're up for the job?"

33

Hospital food sucks. It takes a considerable amount of whining and browbeating to wear Stephen down to the point where he agrees to spring me.

"It's not like I can rely on your common sense to keep you out of trouble," he says. "But if you insist, I can let you go if you promise to take it easy."

"I will. Scout's honor."

"You were never a Boy Scout, Austin," Stephen sighs. "I'll have the nurse get the paperwork rolling."

I head to the bathroom to change into the clothes I was wearing the night they brought me in. They're wrinkled, bloodstained, and dirty as hell, but at least they're mine.

"You're a handsome devil. What's your name?"

I recite the line from one of my favorite movies, *Gross Pointe Blank*, but the reflection in the mirror doesn't respond. I emerge from the bathroom and stride toward the hospital bed.

Over the past twenty-four hours, half of the island has paraded through my hospital room, checking to make sure that I was okay. Everyone, except Ellie. I haven't seen her since she entrusted me to Nico's care. I've spent hours thinking about her. Willing her to come.

But all the excuses I've made for her absence—paperwork, follow up, and the kind of in-depth investigation that goes into an officer-involved shooting—don't hold water.

The nurse arrives with the paperwork and I sign on the dotted line.

Rob picks me up in the Mustang and drives me to the Willows.

"I'm sorry about your car, man."

His car was parked outside my mother's house the night of the fire. By the time the firemen arrived, it was beyond saving.

"Ah, you did me a favor. The transmission was going. Insurance will pay me more than it was worth."

I hope he's telling the truth. He brushes away my offer to keep the Mustang until he can buy another car. We wait in the bar until his wife picks him up. I half expect to find my belongings balled up into the Star Store bag and stuffed behind the counter, like I'm some homeless dude. I'm delighted to find that under orders from Leigh, they've kept my room for me.

The slow climb to the second floor makes my head pound. Inside the room, I rummage for the small vial of pills Stephen prescribed. I pop one and wash it down with an airplane-sized bottle of bourbon I picked up at the Star Store. Man, that place has everything.

The pristine bed looks inviting and I would dearly love a nap, but the sight of Deception Bay out my window beckons me. The sky is overcast. Slate gray waves roil across the Sound and I find myself gazing across the churning water to where Scott's boat went down. I am haunted by the thoughts of what his final moments must have been like. Shocked by Blake's betrayal. How he must have struggled —fought to survive.

Scott was a fighter. Unlike me. I've always been the type to walk away. But I didn't walk away from Blake. In those final moments, I was like my brother, ready to fight for those I love—for the truth.

It's that thought that sends me back out the door with car keys in hand. It would be easy to let all of this go and return to my old life in New York, like none of this had ever happened. But I can't. I'm not the same person who boarded the plane a few weeks ago.

I'm not going to bury my feelings and run away this time without a fight.

It's fully dark by the time I pull off the highway and down the windy road toward Ellie's place. Her bungalow is located near the end of the row. The windows are dark, but her car is in the driveway and I think that maybe she's out back or gone for a run.

The whole way over, I've been practicing my speech. She's amazing—like no other woman I've ever met. She's smart, and brave, and though I know I blew it, that I don't deserve her, there's a tiny part of me that dares to hope that she feels something for me too.

With every fiber of my being, I cling to that hope as I pull into her driveway. At the last second, I see a flash of green eyes.

At first, I think it's a raccoon. Those little furry scavengers are all over the island. But quickly I realize that whatever it is is bigger—not big enough to be a deer but...

Oh, no.

Killer.

The heavy weight of dread presses down on me as I slam the car into park and head toward Ellie's dog. I hear a soft whimper. She wiggles and yelps, tries to get up, but can't. Her fur is matted with blood. A sick feeling washes over me as I realize how badly she is hurt. I place my hand on her head in a gesture of comfort. A high-pitched whine escapes her.

"Hang on. I'll get help."

I'm afraid that lifting her might make her injuries worse, so, leaving her where she is, I rush to the front door. I pound on it hard enough to piss off the neighbors. When Ellie doesn't answer, I round the side of the house. Slip on the stones. Swear.

With every stride, the shooting pain in my head grows more intense. I clench my teeth and keep going, driven on by dread thundering inside me. Something is very wrong.

The backdoor is unlocked, and I let myself inside. My stomach drops. Everywhere I look, I see signs of a struggle.

"Ellie!"

I remind myself that she's a trained police officer—not the kind of person who would be overpowered in a home invasion but... Then I see it. Confetti. Pink and yellow scattered on the floor. I hunker down for a closer look. There are numbers inscribed on each piece. Letters.

They're from a taser.

Oh, god. Ellie.

I search for her phone. Ellie would have a landline. I call 911.

"What's your emergency?" the operator asks.

"This is Austin Martell. I'm at Ellie's house—Chief Sharpe's. There's been a struggle. Her dog has been injured."

"Slow down Mr. Martell and tell me—"

"Send the police. Ellie's gone."

I press my hand into my forehead, as if that could stop the pounding. Behind my eyes, I see a flash of red. Red wine. Red dress. Red blood. The smell of red flowers wafting up from a garden. And all at once, I know.

"Carley! It's Carley."

"Mr. Martell, are you there?"

"Find Carley Darling," I shout into the phone.

34

I leave Daisy there. I don't want to, but help is on the way, and right now, I have got to find Ellie. Keeping one eye on the road, I fumble with my phone until I find Stephen's number.

"You call this resting?"

"Christ, Stephen—"

"There's so much noise I can barely hear you."

"I'm calling from the car. Ellie's dog's been hit."

"What?"

"Her dog. Her German Shepherd. Daisy. She needs help."

"I'm not a vet. I can't—"

"Don't tell me what you can't do. Just get there."

"Austin—"

I hang up.

Rob tried to warn me that Carley was dangerous, but I laughed it off. I'm driving like a man with a death wish down the twisty narrow roads on pure adrenaline, toward the house Carley took me to. The big one on the water. Creepy as shit.

Intuitively, I know I'm right as I slam my foot down on the accelerator and head west.

The good thing about this godforsaken island is that it's not all that big. I'm ten minutes away from my destination. Maybe five.

I take the turn too fast. My tires skid on the gravel, and I crank on the wheel and accelerate into the curve. The black ribbon of asphalt cuts through the dense forest as I race toward Useless Bay.

The full moon casts a silvery glow across the hulking outline of the deserted mansion. My hopes plummet. The windows are dark. Then I spot the Karmann Ghia and know that at least my author instincts are still working.

She's here.

The front door is locked, so I follow the wraparound deck around to the back of the house, glancing through the windows I pass, hoping to catch a glimpse of where they might be. There are no signs of life inside. The kitchen door is unlocked. Another flash of intuition strikes, and I know it's an invitation.

She wants me to come inside.

This house gave me the willies in full daylight, and now, with only the moon to illuminate the cavernous rooms, the place has all the charm of Bates Motel.

What I wouldn't give for a knife or some other weapon to take with me, but the cupboards are empty. And worse, the sound of the drawers clanging open and shut is enough to rouse the dead. The fruitless search is taking too long. I'm going to have to wing it.

The corridor is pitch black. I hold my hands out in front of me and try to recall the layout of the house. To the right of the kitchen is the dining room. I pause in the doorway and listen. The place is as silent as a tomb. I keep going.

No matter how softly I tread down the corridor toward the grand entrance, my footsteps echo in the vast space. If Carley is hiding on the first floor, she will have plenty of warning. I peek through a doorway. Moonlight spills through the windows, casting ghostly shadows over the great room. It looks as empty as the rest of the main floor.

There's a reason I write cozy romances and not thrillers. I don't consider myself a coward, but the thought of hunting through the second floor waiting for a knife-wielding maniac to jump out of the dark makes my skin crawl. But if Ellie's up there, I have to find her.

Steeling myself, I exit the great room and ease toward the curved staircase off the grand entrance. My foot touches the first stair. A sound stops me dead. It's thin. High-pitched. I cock my head toward the upstairs landing and listen. Goosebumps ripple across my skin as I realize what the sound is.

Singing.

A woman is singing. I can't make out the melody as I climb the stairs and follow the sound through the second floor. With every step the singing becomes more distinct, until I can pinpoint its location.

It's coming from the turret room.

Aw, Christ. Of all the scary places in this nightmare of a house, she had to be up there. With every step up the spiral staircase, the singing grows louder. The tune is classic. Timeless. Horrifying.

Rock-a-bye Baby.

"Carley," I call.

The singing stops. I crest the top of the stairs and my breath catches. Tied to a chair like human bait, I see her. *Ellie.*

Her mouth is covered in duct tape. Fear flashes in her eyes. Her gaze shifts away from me to the other end of the room where Carley is standing. Her back is to the stairwell, facing the windows. She's humming under her breath and bouncing something in her arms. Horror-struck, I know what it is.

Oh, shit. A baby.

"Is that Leigh's baby?"

Carley doesn't answer. She turns toward me with a smile that turns my blood to ice. A baby is cradled in one arm. Her free hand holds a gun. I recoil a step. Catch my breath.

"What are you doing, Carley?"

"Waiting for you. I knew you'd come looking for her and when you did..."

She shrugs, as if to say the rest is obvious. Inevitable. I swipe my sweating palms on my jeans and take a step toward her.

"This isn't about her. It's about you and me."

"Of course it's about her. It's always been about *her*. She's taken everything from me—my baby, Scott. She deserves to lose everything, just like I did. And then you came along, and I thought maybe—"

Christ, she's gone full-on Annie Wilkes crazy, right out of her cockadoodie mind.

"Put down the gun."

"I thought I could make you love me. But you don't."

"Ellie's done nothing to you."

"She wants you."

"No, she doesn't. She knows what I am—a shallow, selfish bastard. This is between us. I hurt you, but I can make things right, if you'll let me. Put the gun down. We'll leave here. Go to New York."

A jagged peal of laughter fills the room. Shards of fear impale my heart.

"You expect me to believe that you're not in love with her? Look at you. Look where you're standing."

Carley waves the tip of the gun at me, noting my positioning. Each step I've taken places me between her and Ellie.

"You're willing to trade your life for hers."

"You're not going to shoot anyone. Please, Carley, give me the gun and we can talk this thing through."

"You think I'm stupid? If I put the gun down, you'll leave me, the same way your brother did."

"You're right. Scott wasn't perfect. He shouldn't have used you. He shouldn't have forced you to terminate the pregnancy."

"That was my baby—our baby."

A sheen of tears glimmers in her eyes as she gazes down on the swaddled bundle in her arms. The pain in her voice is as sharp as the edge of a knife. Just as dangerous. She levels the gun at my chest as she rocks the sleeping child. How I wish he would squawk, or cry, do anything that tells me he's alive.

"I know, sweetheart. We've all made mistakes. Scott, Leigh, you, and me most of all. The best we can do is accept the things we've done and learn from them. This—" I gesture toward the child in her arms. "Hurting Leigh's baby won't bring your child back."

"She doesn't deserve a child."

"Please, may I hold him?"

"Why?"

"Because he's innocent. He's done nothing."

Carley chokes out a bitter laugh.

"She named him Scott. And you think I'm sick?"

There must be some way to get through to her—something I can say that gets everybody out of here alive, but what? I'm staring at the gun in her hand, thinking that if I could just knock it out of her hand...

As if reading my intent, Carley steps back. I glance over my shoulder at Ellie. Our gazes lock. She gives her head a tiny shake. A warning. I turn back toward Carley.

"You're not sick. You're hurt. Let me help you."

"Liar. You're such a liar. It's too late. You can save her or the baby. You choose."

A cold terror grips me. I stare at the baby cradled in her arms. It's an impossible choice. Ellie is screaming through the duct tape. I hear the clang of her chair rocking from side to side.

My heart stops as Carley darts around me and points the gun at Ellie. I don't think, I don't breathe as I block her shot.

"Her?"

The toxic word spews from her mouth as she hoists the baby high. I scream as she lets go. Blankets flutter in the air. I lunge toward the falling baby, hands outstretched, praying I get there before he hits the floor.

The gun goes off in an ear-splitting crack. The bullet grazes past me as the bundle lands in my palms. The moment I touch it, I know that something's wrong. He's too light. He's...

A doll?

I feel an anguished stab of dread as I spin toward Ellie. She is slumped in the chair. She's been hit. A thick puddle of blood pools beneath her chair.

Tears glitter in Carley's tortured eyes. The tip of the gun is pressed into the soft flesh beneath her chin.

"Carley, no..."

"It's too late," she says.

There's no time to scream when the final gunshot roars.

35

There's a reason I didn't become a surgeon. Getting sick at the sight of blood is only part of it. At the best of times, my hands have never been particularly steady, and right now they are shaking so badly that I can barely free Ellie from the chair. It's a small blessing that she's not conscious to witness this stunning display of manliness.

"Please, Ellie. Please don't die on me. I love you."

My heart thunders as I search for Ellie's wound. It's not hard to find.

Blood saturates her left shoulder. I gather her into my arms and carry her down the spiral staircase. Once this concussion is healed, I swear that I'm going to start some weight training. For real. My arms are trembling, and I'm drenched with sweat by the time I get her outside. And my head... Yellow spots blot my vision when I finally reach the deck.

I carefully set Ellie down and search my pockets for my phone. *I'm such an idiot.* The freaking cell is in the car.

Gasping to catch my breath, I stumble for the stairs. A distant sound stops me. Sirens? For a second, I wonder if I've passed out and

I'm dreaming that the cavalry is coming to save us. Then I see them cut through the dark. Flashing lights. Racing toward the beach.

A profound sense of relief crashes over me and I return to Ellie's side. My hands are pressed against her wounded shoulder as a swarm of cops and firemen descend upon us.

They shove me aside and tend to Ellie. I scooch back against the railing and press my palms against my eyes. I breathe. The cacophony of questions they hurl my way amplifies the blistering pain inside my head.

"You!" a cop shouts at me. "Is the shooter still in there?"

I give a dull nod. "She's dead."

I don't know that for sure. I didn't exactly check.

Weapons drawn, the cops enter the house. More flashing lights slash through the darkness as the ambulance arrives. I recognize the EMT from the Willows—Nico. He and another EMT waste no time in loading Ellie onto a gurney and whisking her away.

I watch the ambulance disappear. With each breath, I am willing Ellie strength. It's the closest I can come to a prayer.

"You okay?" someone asks. It's O'Brien.

"Yeah. How did you...find us?"

"You might be shocked to learn that we islanders are trained in state-of-the-art law enforcement techniques."

"Yeah?"

"We pinged her phone."

The unexpected simplicity of his response makes me laugh. The laughing makes the pain in my head worse, but I don't care. After the hellish night I've endured, it's either laughter or tears.

O'Brien drives me to the hospital, where Stephen waits. A shard of pain twists in my heart at the sight of his blood-stained scrubs.

"Ellie?"

"She's in surgery."

I will never forgive myself if something happens to her. If it weren't for me, Carley wouldn't have come after her. Stephen reads my expression and squeezes my shoulder.

"She's going to be okay. And so is her dog. A friend of mine, who actually is a vet, is taking care of her."

"Thank you."

"Yeah, yeah," he says. "The way I hear it, you're the hero."

The word "hero" rings false in my ears and I slowly shake my head.

"I couldn't stop Carley…"

"I know. You did your best, but Carley was deeply troubled."

My legs feel wooden as I follow Stephen inside.

"We're going to start charging you rent soon," I hear him say as I stretch out on the lumpy hospital mattress and pass out.

It's barely dawn when the nurse comes in to check on me. A few hours later, I'm awoken again by the arrival of my breakfast tray.

Back home, I'd consider this low-grade dog food, but today I wolf it down.

A few hours later, I go in search of Ellie's room. It's not hard to find. I follow the throng of cops down the hall and linger outside the door until the last of them are gone. Only then do I venture inside.

I don't make it past the door when the bottom drops out of my world. Ellie's not alone. Greg is there. He's perched beside her on the bed, looking at her in a way that makes my heart sink.

I meant it when I told Ellie that I loved her. The way I feel about her is like nothing I've experienced before. I would do anything for a chance to prove myself to her.

But how's that going to work when I am three thousand miles away? Her life is on Whidbey, and mine… What could I possibly have to offer her that would justify taking her away from a place she loves, a job she loves?

And that's if she's not serious about Greg and if she feels anything for me besides disdain. I mean really…I haven't exactly been the kind of guy she could rely on. Not like Greg, who probably jumped the first ferry so he could be here by her side.

That's the kind of guy she deserves. Someone who puts her first. Someone who's not selfish. Self-absorbed.

Maybe I could convince her to give me a shot. Maybe I could even convince her that I love her. But those are just words. If I truly love her, I would want what's best for her. And can I honestly say that's me?

She belongs here, and me? I don't belong anywhere.

It doesn't take long to wrap up final affairs. After the fire, there's not much to pack. I spend a good ten minutes staring at the blackened remains of my mother's house. Eventually, I'll need to figure out what to do with it, but that's a problem for another day.

I turn back toward the car. That's when I hear it. Him.

A gray streak comes bolting out of the wreckage heading straight for me. I gape, in open-mouthed shock, at Cato's skinny form. I shake my head and scoop him up.

"You are truly indestructible," I tell him.

He yowls in response. Now I have one more stop to make before I hit the ferry. The Star Store sells cat carriers. Of course, they do. They have everything.

Hours later, with Cato safely onboard, I'm on a plane bound for New York.

At last.

EPILOGUE

The heat from the studio lights warms my face. A burst of adrenaline shoots through me as I settle into the guest chair, opposite Felicity Kane, host of the most popular entertainment news program on the planet. She shakes her blonde hair off her shoulders and directs her smile at the camera.

"You've all seen the story on the news. Today, Austin Martell is here to tell us about his new book—a gripping true crime thriller about sex, lies, and murder. Welcome to the show, Austin."

"Thank you, Felicity. It's good to be here."

"Wow, your book is really killing it."

"Ha, I see what you did there," I joke with a grin.

The audience erupts in laughter and Felicity beams.

"Your mystery books have been bestsellers before, but this one—" Felicity presses her hand to her chest and lets out a breath. "Whew. It was a heart-stopper. How did it feel to be caught up in the middle of a real-life murder mystery?"

"You know what they say, whatever doesn't kill you leaves facial scars." I run my fingers across a jagged line of scar tissue on my forehead, a souvenir from my ordeal. "To tell you the truth, Felicity, I would rather write murder mysteries than live through them."

"Your brother was killed by his best friend, who made his death look like a tragic accident—a drowning at sea. The only one who knew the truth was the man who investigated the boat accident. Instead of telling the police what he found, he extorted money from the killer—Blake Parsons."

"Mark Hammer underestimated the gravity of the situation. Blake knew that if the truth about my brother's death was revealed it would destroy his family—his life."

Felicity leans in with a serious expression on her face. "Parsons attacked your mother in her own home because he believed Hammer had sent her evidence that implicated him in your brother's murder."

"That threat set the two of them on a collision course with death."

"A collision course with death," Felicity repeats with feigned gravity. "I was shocked and saddened when I read how your mother died. Can you tell us about her, Austin?"

Months have gone by, and still, I feel the weight of sadness press down on me at the thought of my mother's senseless death.

"I wish I could say we were close, but the truth was, we barely communicated. Like many families, ours was far from ideal. We were both too proud to let go of the pain we'd caused each other—the wounds we sustained over my brother's death. But here's the thing— you never know how much time you have with those you love. I missed out on the relationship I could have had with my mother, if only I had found a way to forgive her."

"That's one of the messages of this book, isn't it? Forgiveness."

"I realize now that she did the best she could—that in her own way, she loved me, and I loved her. I wish I'd had a chance to tell her that."

A hush falls over the audience. A mist of tears forms over my eyes and I blink them away.

"Love. That brings me to Parsons's accomplice—Carley Darling. She was in love with you."

I cringe at Felicity's characterization and shake my head.

"Obsession is not the same thing as love. Carley was damaged. She needed help. Tragically, Blake exploited her illness and manipulated her into helping him kill Mark Hammer and set fire to my mother's home."

"With you inside." Felicity shivers as if disturbed by the thought. "But for me, the most chilling part of the story comes when Carley kidnaps the chief of police, Ellie Sharpe. Rumor has it that there was more going on between the two of you than just crime solving. What's the real story, Austin?"

She cocks an eyebrow and shoots me a curious look.

"Now, Felicity, what kind of mystery author would I be if I revealed all of my secrets?"

"Are you saying that you're not in love with her?"

I let out a breath and open my hands in a shrug,

"Ellie's life is on Whidbey Island, and me...I'm afraid I'm destined to be a cliché...a bachelor with a New York condo and a cat."

"And one hell of a movie deal," she says.

Felicity wraps up the interview while backstage Diana waits.

"Way to go, rockstar," she says. "Twitter is blowing up after that interview."

She scrolls through her Twitter feed with a gleeful grin, but I couldn't care less. For all my bravado, a bone-deep weariness crashes over me as I collapse into a nearby chair.

"We should celebrate. Drinks are on me," Diana says.

There was a time when I would have liked nothing better, but I was a different person then.

"I just want to go home," I say.

That was three months ago, and I've barely left the condo since. As far as excuses go, I've got a good one. I've been working on the next book. Even Diana can't argue with that. But as dusk gives way to the dead of night, I set my laptop down on the coffee table. Stretching my arms above my head, I stand.

It's late. The rhythm of the city moves outside my window. I press my palm flat against the glass and stare out at the mass of humanity moving like ants through the Manhattan streets. I used to love the pulsing city lights, the hum of traffic, everything about this place, but now it feels fake, artificial—all the beauty and none of the heart. I find myself missing the wide open sky and the sound of the sea, the herons.

I miss Ellie.

From the kitchen, Cato yowls for his dinner. I run my hands through my hair and turn away from the window. I think of Ellie and Carley and everything that happened—how different things could have been if only...

I could play the "if only" game forever.

Inside the kitchen, Cato circles his dish, and I give him a half-hearted smile. He brushes up against my leg as I open a tin of food. Returning to the living room, I stare at my open laptop. And with sudden and complete clarity I know what I must do.

The lobby of Writer's Place Literary Agency is as quiet as a mortuary this time of the morning. The receptionist perks up when she sees me come ambling down the hall.

"Good morning, Mr. Martell. Was Ms. Black expecting you?"

I shake my head and hand her a flash drive.

"Could you give Diana this?"

"Of course."

I smile as I picture the look on Diana's face when she opens the file and realizes what I've done. I wonder how long it will take her to call me. Two pages? Maybe three? By then Cato and I will be long gone with nothing but rainbows and sunshine in our future.

THE SKY BLAZES a brilliant orange outside the jetliner's window. I drink in the beauty of the snowcapped peaks of the Cascade Mountain Range below.

"You were really out," the big guy in the seat beside me says.

Passengers fidget in their seats, anxious to disembark. Six hours crammed into a tiny space is five hours too long.

"I don't think I've slept that well in years."

"On vacation?" he asks.

I shake my head. "Going home."

Following the throng of swarming humanity toward baggage claim, I check my phone. Diana's left a dozen messages. The shrill tone of the first is about what I expected, and I listen with a smirk.

"Austin, what the hell is this?"

I delete the first message without listening to it all the way through and skip to the last.

"A thriller? I hate you," she says, not meaning a word of it. I can hear the smile in her voice. "You kept me up all night reading. Quite honestly, it's the best thing you've ever written, although I have no idea how I'm going to brand it. I guess that's why I get paid the big bucks. Call me."

THOUGH THE RAIN HAS STOPPED, it's cold and damp. Gulls swoop through the marine layer and skim across the silvery waters of Puget Sound. Steam spirals up from my coffee cup into the briny air.

I see her outline in the mist. Coming toward me. Running down the beach in long, fluid strides. A fresh bout of nerves assaults me. I set the coffee cup down and stand. I should have brought dog treats.

"Killer."

Her ears twitch up and she raises her snout into the air. A fin of fur stands between her shoulder blades and I fight the urge to recoil. I shake off my fear and stretch out my hand. Who needs all ten fingers anyway?

"Is that any way to greet the guy who saved your life?"

Daisy sniffs and wags her tail. Suddenly, I can breathe. The moment of relief is short-lived, though, as the shadow of another form approaches. Ellie slows as she catches sight of me. She stops a few feet away. Daisy stands by my side.

"Traitor," she says to the dog.

Daisy abandons me and trots toward Ellie, still wagging her tail. I jam my fists into my pockets.

"Hi," I say.

Now that I'm here, I've completely lost my swagger. Nothing has ever mattered this much, and I'm afraid of screwing it up. But I've got to do this—I've got to tell her how I feel before I lose my nerve.

"Look, I know that I completely messed things up between us. Not that there really was an 'us,' but..."

Oh, man. This is the worst first draft ever. I've spent months thinking about what I would say to Ellie. But now that I'm standing here staring down into her face, my carefully rehearsed speech has fled from my mind and left me fumbling for words like an idiot.

"My life in New York has never felt so empty—like there's a part of me that's missing. I love you, Ellie. I do. And I don't know where things stand between you and Greg, but if you're willing to give me a chance—"

That's as far as I get before Ellie puts me out of my misery. She closes the gap between us and presses her lips against mine. And suddenly everything I wanted to say doesn't matter, and there is only her.

I pull her close and lose myself in the feel of her lips, the taste of her mouth, the way her body fits against mine. My heart soars as we kiss, and I swear that I have never experienced a more perfect moment. I don't want it to end.

Daisy has other ideas. She wedges her snout between us and lets out a whine. Laughing, we break apart. I place my hand on Daisy's back and rest my forehead against Ellie's.

"Well, I do have to admit that things have been positively boring since you left," she says.

"Is that so?"

"No homicidal maniacs running around the island. No kidnappings. If this keeps up, I could find myself out of a job."

"We can't have that," I joke.

Waves lap against the stony shore as we stroll toward the house hand in hand. The mist off the water wraps around us, and I am filled with a profound sense of peace. Belonging.

Ellie stops as we reach the stairs leading to her deck. I gaze down into her eyes. I want to memorize this moment and carry it with me, always.

"The other morning, I was watching the sun come up and I realized something."

"You were still drunk?"

"Funny, but no. From the moment my plane touched down at LaGuardia, all I've wanted to do is to come home."

"To Whidbey?"

"No, Ellie. To you."

AFTERWORD

Dear Reader,

Thank you for reading DECEPTION BAY. My friend Stella once said, "You're funny. You should write something funny." Much easier said than done. Still. I had a blast writing from Austin's point of view. So thanks Dad for the twisted sense of humor. I finally put it to good use.

If you enjoyed the story, please consider posting a review. We writers love that kind of thing. Like Austin, connecting with readers is one of my favorite things to do. You can find me on Facebook at: https://www.facebook.com/authorchrispatchell/

To keep up on my crazy author happenings, you can sign up for my newsletter at: www.chrispatchell.com.

Until next time.

ALSO BY CHRIS PATCHELL

DEADLY LIES

VOW OF SILENCE

IN THE DARK

DARK HARVEST

Made in the USA
Columbia, SC
26 October 2021

47621556R00133